IT'S
THE END OF
THE WORLD
AS I
KNOW IT

MATTHEW LANDIS

DIAL BOOKS FOR YOUNG READERS

To my students who have lived this story

DIAL BOOKS FOR YOUNG READERS
An imprint of Penguin Random House LLC, New York

Copyright © 2019 by Matthew Landis.

Visit us online at penguinrandomhouse.com

Printed and bound in Canada
ISBN 9780735228016

1 3 5 7 9 10 8 6 4 2

Design by Mina Chung
Text set in Perrywood MT Std

THE PAST IS LONG
AND THE FUTURE IS SHORT.

—*THE AGE OF MIRACLES*, Karen Thompson Walker

1

"**S**o what did you say?" I ask Tommy.

He hands me another screw and I send it through the plywood with my cordless drill. "I said, 'Mother: No, thank you.'"

"He said, 'Not happening, Kelly,'" Brock calls behind us. He's loafing in the shade of the giant maple tree in my backyard, murdering flies with his tree trunk arms. "And then she said, 'Don't call me by my first name, because I birthed you and therefore control your life.'"

"She's making me try out." Tommy sneezes three times in a row because of his massive allergies. "For soccer."

I get my level out and make sure the plywood is lined up straight with the shed wall. "Hmm. Soccer is pretty much just running," I say. "Probably ninety percent running."

"I know," Tommy says. His arm bumps into me when he says it. He's always talking up in your personal space. "But she threatened to sell Pete."

"She always does that. She won't actually do it."

"She posted him on Snake4Sale.com," Brock says. "Tommy cried."

"I didn't cry." Tommy heads to the shade and slumps on the ground next to Brock, which makes him look extra small. Me and Tommy both have brown hair and people used to say we could be brothers until I grew way bigger last summer. "It was, like, a moaning sound."

"Sounded like crying," Brock says.

I pull a screwdriver from my tool belt and start checking the tension on each screw. If they're too tight, they could crack the plywood under the extra pressure from people banging on the outside to get in. "You should pretend to be sick for tryouts."

"Kelly will know," Tommy says. "She has, like, psychic mom powers."

"Kelly knows all," Brock says.

Tommy fishes out a Gatorade from the cooler. "But it's fine, because I won't, like, make the team. I'll get cut on the first day of tryouts. And Pete will be saved."

"Pete wants to eat you," Brock says. "He tried once and he's going to try again. Let her sell him."

"That was a misunderstanding," Tommy says. "Pete was confused. He thought my hand was a mouse."

"I think to Pete, we're all mice," I say. "He's a python."

"No. You guys." Tommy shakes his head. "Pete is cool."

"There is a predator living in your house and he is coming for you," Brock says.

The alarm on my watch goes off. It's one of those big bulky ones with all the buttons you see Navy Seals wear on TV. The doomsday blog I follow, *Apocalypse Soon!,* gave it ten out of ten mushroom clouds.

"I will push the earth out of orbit," I say, taking off my tool belt. "Witness me."

I toss my watch to Brock and he counts down, "Three, two, one . . . destroy gravity."

I drop to the grass and crank out thirty pushups before my arms start to burn. At forty, I slow down. Five more and my shoulders are screaming. I close my eyes and do smaller sets of two and three. My muscles are lead but I keep pushing. Blood pounds in my ears and the sun blazes on me like the fire that will spew out of the supervolcano under Yellowstone National Park on September 21.

"Time," Brocks says.

I collapse onto the spikey grass. "How many?"

"Sixty-five," Tommy says. "New record."

I jump up and beat my chest with dead arms. Six months ago I couldn't do twenty pushups in a day, and now I'm closing in on seventy in two minutes.

I'm getting stronger. I will be ready.

Brock throws my watch back. "My mom wants me to play football," he says. "I heard her talking to my dad about it. They think if I don't exercise, I will become part of the couch." He slow tracks a fly in the air but lets it go. Brock is deadly, but he can also show mercy.

"Wanna go out for soccer with me?" Tommy asks him. "We could get cut together."

"I have Hall Monitor training after school."

"They have training for that?" I ask.

"One of the many changes I suggested as Hall Monitor in Chief."

"Dee." Tommy comes over and gets real close again. He waits a few seconds and then says, "You wanna do it? It would be like when we did tee-ball but just ate sunflower seeds on the bench."

I look at the shed and think of all the stuff I have to do still: Hang the rest of the plywood. Order the gas masks. Mainly it's the rolling steel door I'm worried about. That thing was supposed to come two weeks ago, but there was a shipping mess-up.

"Can't. You know—the apocalypse."

He sneezes five times. "Yeah."

Clang.

We look two backyards over and see my neighbor Misty walking toward a tree with a paper target on it. She digs around in the grass and picks up a hatchet, then walks back to her spot. Throws again.

Clang.

It bounces off the tree way above the target.

"What," Brock says, "in the crap."

"At least she's hitting the tree now," I say. "She's been out there for a week."

"I thought she was sick," Tommy says. "She missed most of school last year."

I shrug. "I don't know."

We watch Misty take off her Phillies hat and fix her ponytail. She goes through a bunch of weird stretches, really taking her time lining up the shot.

"She doesn't look sick," Brock says. "She looks ready to hatchet murder that tree."

"I think it was cancer," Tommy says.

"No," I say. "It was something else. My sister knows her sister and she told me, but I forget."

Misty lets it fly, and the hatchet sails through the air perfectly, like in a movie.

Thunk.

It sticks dead center in the target.

Bull's-eye.

"Whoa," Tommy says.

Misty shrieks and runs to the tree. She's jumping around and celebrating. Now she sees us and shouts, *"Did you see that? Please tell me you saw that!"*

Brock gives her a thumbs-up. "Nice."

"Ohmygosh!" Misty shouts, and it's all joy and she's got this smile like the sun. She screams again.

Her mom whips open the sliding glass door and runs out onto their deck yelling, *"Mercedes!* What's wrong?"

"Look at this!" Misty points to the tree. *"Can you believe this? Bull's. Eye!"*

Her mom looks at us. Tommy waves.

"Look at it!"

Brock stands up and says, "Mrs. Knoll: We will all testify to that bull's-eye."

Her mom makes a face like *I am sort of embarrassed and also confused* and goes back inside.

"Yes!" Misty shrieks. She puts the hatchet and paper target in one of those red wagons little kids get hauled around in. She pulls it across her yard and points at us, shouting, *"Amazing!"*

"That girl is, like, off," Tommy says.

She walks between her house and the Mitchells', the people next to me. The wagon rolls pretty good on the grass, like it could carry something way heavier and not be a problem.

"Yeah, she's weird," I say.

"But she has hatchet skills," Brock says. He claps his hands above his head and shows us the dragonfly he just executed. "That's a good person to have around."

2

My sister, Claudia, drops the laundry basket onto the family room floor to make sure I hear her. "For someone who's so good at putting stuff together, you really stink at keeping your room from falling apart. Something literally died in there. You need to clean it before school starts tomorrow."

"Mmhm."

"And seriously—take off your work boots when you're in the house. I've said that like a million times."

I'm at the kitchen island, inhaling Cheez-Its and scrolling through Amazon's list of gas masks. Some guys on *Apocalypse Soon!* say the ACME Israeli mask is the best, but there's another bunch of guys who say this other one is better.

"Okay," I say.

"Dee, I'm serious."

"Clean my room. Got it."

"And work boots."

"Uh-huh."

Claudia lets out this big sigh and starts folding laundry on the couch. "I don't ask you to do anything around here. All I'm asking is that you clean your stupid room. I'm the one sorting through trash and underwear so you have clothes to wear."

"Sorry."

"Don't be sorry. Just clean your room."

"Okay." I click on the Israeli gas mask and read the reviews. All five stars. Some guy said he tested it by setting off a smoke bomb in his woodshed and the mask totally worked. "I need Dad's credit card."

"For what?"

"Gas masks."

Claudia gives me a face like *Derrick, you are crazy.*

"I have the cash to pay him from all the decks I fixed this summer," I say. "I just need the card to buy it. He takes it out of my savings account."

"Clean your room and I'll give it to you," she says.

"Give it to me and I'll clean my room."

"I'm not an idiot."

"Are you sure?"

"Derrick." Sounds like she's clenching her teeth. "I'm not giving it to you until you clean your room."

I shove some more Cheez-Its in my mouth. "I'll just get it from him when he comes home."

Claudia shrieks.

Ugh.

Last time we fought like this, she didn't do my laundry for a month.

Not good.

I take off my work boots and put them in the garage. I

join her on the couch and we fold for a while. She keeps refolding the ones I've already done.

"Why are you doing that?" I ask.

"You didn't do it right." She holds up my T-shirt and starts folding it again. "This is how She did it."

I give up and just sit there. I can see the shed through the family room window and picture which bin I'll put the gas masks in when they get here. And what's the deal with my steel door? What if it doesn't get here in time? My hands start to do this buzzing thing, so I make really tight fists and then let go like Dr. Mike taught me.

"Dee," Claudia finally says, "this is a big year, okay? I've got college applications due next month, AP classes, and all the stuff going on here. I can't battle with you like this."

"Yeah," I say. "Plus all your boyfriends."

"Did you just make a joke?"

"I can be funny. People say I'm hilarious."

"You used to be," she says, sort of quiet.

I need to get the heck out of here. "I'll go clean my room."

It takes me an hour of putting stuff away until I can see the floor. The thing that smelled like death was a cereal bowl with milk still in it. Claudia drops my laundry basket off and puts the credit card on top. Truce.

After I order the masks, I grab the super-thick *Survival Guide Handbook: A Guide for When Help Is Not on the Way* and head out to the shed. I lie on the cot and reread the section on basic medical supplies, checking it against the list that's hanging on the wall near my med kit. My hands start buzzing again when I can't find the fish amoxicillin I got off eBay, but then I see it in the corner of the bag, and it goes away. Dr. Mike, this professional head examiner I used to see, said stress can make your body do weird stuff, and that if I start to feel dizzy I should just relax and breathe through my nose. But that's stupid because if I'm getting dizzy I'm gonna be totally freaking out and gulping air as fast as I can so that I don't pass out from all the stress that's making me dizzy.

I go out and move two cinder blocks to the other side of the shed. I drag a piece of plywood around and put it on the cinder blocks so the top lines up just under the roof. Once I check to make sure it's straight, I put four screws on each edge. I do the same on the back side with my last piece of plywood, but the ground is tilted, so it takes me longer to get it level.

It's just getting dark when my dad's truck pulls in. His headlights swing across the yard and shine on me and the shed for a few seconds before he cuts the ignition. He's on his phone because construction bosses are always on their phones. He waves to me on his way inside and I sort of wave back.

I put my tools inside the shed and do another inventory because double-checking = survival. The opposite wall is a year's supply of MREs—meals ready to eat—which is basically dehydrated food that army guys eat when they're at war. My water cases take up the corners nearest the door. If I have to ration them, I could probably last a year and a half in here. In another corner are some crates with my medical equipment, batteries, and backup flashlights, and four hazmat suits (plus another one inside the go bag in my bedroom). Just missing those gas masks.

And that rolling steel door.

My phone buzzes. It's Tommy texting *Hey Brock is here come over.* I start typing and then delete it. He says *U coming?* and I stare at the screen until it goes dark, pretty much like the world is going to go dark. The End is coming and my friends don't care.

Nobody cares.

I lie down on the cot and close my eyes. The movie

in my head starts like somebody hit a giant PLAY button.

I'm in a desert with mountains all around. It's not hot, which is weird, because this is a desert, and the sky is blue. No clouds. I'm standing on a dirt road and now it's rumbling under my feet, like an earthquake. Now lava is spewing out the mountaintops and running hard down the slopes and everything is on fire. The buzzing in my hands creeps up my arms to my face, like fire ants aiming for my brain. I grab the cot frame because the shed is spinning and try to breathe through my nose. Dr. Mike said I'm really good at tricking my body into thinking there's an emergency by obsessing about The End and that if I stop doing that, I won't have as many freak-outs.

But I won't stop because it's not a trick. There will be an emergency on September 21. Probably a million different emergencies all connected to The Big One.

The End.

I roll to the floor and push the earth. Instead of counting, I run through the basic first aid. The buzzing goes away, but my face feels so hot and there's tons of sweat. I crank out another twenty pushups before collapsing.

I lie with my back against the floorboards. My head rolls to the side and I see this dark knot of wood sticking out from behind a food bin. I stare at it for a while and wonder why some idiot shed maker guy didn't use a clean piece of wood. I look up at the hanging LED light until my eyes water, then I close the place down and walk outside.

"Hey."

I jump.

Misty comes out of nowhere wearing a bike helmet. Everything smells like sunscreen.

"Hey," I say.

"Sorry I scared you."

"It's okay."

"Do you have a bike pump?"

"What?"

Misty mimes pumping up a tire with both arms. "Bike pump."

"Uh. Yeah."

"Can I borrow it?"

"Sure."

"Sweet."

I walk around to the garage and open it. Is she going to the beach? Smells like it. I dig out the pump from behind a snow shovel and give it to her.

"Awesome," she says.

"You shouldn't ride bikes at night. You could get hit by a car."

"Yeah." She looks at me for a second. "You okay?"

"Huh?"

"You're all sweaty and breathing hard."

I wipe my face with my sleeve. "I was doing pushups."

She looks at the shed, then back at me. Messes with the bike pump a little. "You see that bull's-eye?"

"Yeah," I say, and she smiles. It takes up her whole face and I'm smiling too, and it's not that awkward. There's this weird feeling like we've done this before.

And then she walks back to her house.

04 SEPTEMBER TUESDAY

18 DAYS BEFORE THE END

1

"**G**et some breakfast?" my dad asks me.

I grab Pop-Tarts from the pantry and shove them in my pocket. "Yeah."

"Lunch?"

"I'm buying."

"Do you need money?"

"Claudia prepaid for the whole year," I say, which was stupid because I won't be eating lunch at school for very long.

"Oh, right."

Claudia comes in the kitchen and pulls a hunk of chicken out of the freezer. "I'm grilling this tonight, so don't pig out with the guys after work." He raises his coffee to toast her. She snatches the Oreo from him and chucks it in the trash. "Heart disease is a real thing. Dinner at six."

"Got it."

She kisses his cheek. "Bye."

"Love you."

Claudia grabs the keys and asks me, "Did you text them?"

"Yeah," I say. "They're ready."

"One second late and they're back to taking the bus. I cannot be late this year."

"They know the new rules."

"Have a good first day, buddy," my dad says.

I nod.

We throw our stuff in the trunk of Claudia's Subaru wagon. I sit in the back because I don't want to stare at that stupid Air Force sticker on the glove compartment she won't take off.

"You could be nice," she says, backing out of the driveway. "He's trying."

I see Misty and her sister climbing into their car. I guess she survived night biking. "Trying to what?"

"To connect. Father-son stuff."

"Okay, Dr. Mike."

"You know what I mean. I'm not saying you have to go on a camping trip with him, but you don't have to be such a jerk."

"Maybe I'm a jerk."

"No," she says. "You're not."

"Maybe I don't have a lot to say."

"Think of something."

I roll down the window and put my hand out. It's already humid and the *Apocalypse Soon!* weather alert on my phone says it's going to be 91. There's a legit chance Tommy dies of dehydration at soccer tryouts.

"You know he talks about us on those Internet dating sites," I say. "He didn't log out of his email once and I saw it. He was talking about us to one of those women."

Claudia cranks up the AC. "So?"

"So?"

She turns down the next street toward Tommy's house. "He has to talk to someone, and it's not going to be me. It sure isn't going to be you."

"They all probably hang out in some chat room and laugh at how messed up we are."

"I'm pretty sure that's not happening." Claudia slows at Tommy's driveway. "I think whatever helps him is good."

I grip the door handle and think maybe I could rip the whole thing off if I really tried.

"Bold first day outfit, Brock," Claudia says.

He slaps both of his arms that are sticking out of a neon-green tank top. "The Chief Hall Monitor must be bold. These seventh graders can't find their classes alone."

She smirks at Tommy through the rearview mirror. "And what boarding school am I dropping you off at, Master Thomas?"

He stares down at his brand-new polo shirt tucked into brand-new khaki shorts. "Kelly says I need to make a good first impression."

"Don't worry," Brock says. "I will protect you from any clothing-related bullying."

2

The car line is super-long, so Claudia lets us out by the tennis courts. We walk to the bus loop, Tommy tripping while trying to read his schedule and Brock yelling at some seventh graders. I scan the building and count windows, hoping most of my classes are interior rooms. Wouldn't take much of a windstorm to shatter those things and shower us all with razor-sharp glass.

"Do you smell that?" Brock asks, taking in a big whiff of air as we head inside. "Fear. And deodorant being used for the first time. Some of them are probably using their mom's." He points to a tiny kid sagging under a giant backpack. "You there. Do you need help finding your homeroom?"

"Uhhhhh," the kid says.

"Hall Monitor coming through," Brock yells, guiding the kid down the hallway. "Move it or I will move you with my body."

I point the other way and say, "I got math."

"I have social studies," Tommy says.

"That sucks."

He sneezes once, real big. "It's kind of crazy, like, not being on the same team. We don't have any classes together this year."

The warning bell rings: Three minutes until first period starts.

"See ya, dude," I say.

He waves and heads the other way.

Brock's on Tommy's team, so I lone wolf it through morning classes. All my new teachers say this year is going to be "far more difficult than seventh grade" and they expect "far more personal responsibility," which is exactly what they said last year. On my way back from gym I see Misty hauling a giant instrument case that looks like a violin except the thing is five times her size and almost takes her down before the orchestra teacher shows her how to carry it.

At lunch I grab three slices of pizza and find Tommy and Brock near the back of the cafeteria. They know to sit at the table farthest from the giant glass windows that could become deadly shrapnel.

"I think I might puke," Tommy is telling Brock. "Like, blow chunks."

"Tell him he needs to eat or he's going to faint at tryouts," Brock says to me.

"You need to eat," I say. "Or you're going to faint at tryouts." I shove my tray at him to take some pizza. Tommy bites his nails.

"Then you gotta drink something," Brock says, sliding him some Gatorade. "Electrolyte load."

Tommy takes a sip. "This kid Jack said the first three days are just running and that lots of kids pass out."

"Jack is a doofus," I say. "You'll be fine. Just keep drinking that."

"Boys," says a voice behind us.

"Hey, Mr. Killroy," Brock says.

Our hulking guidance counselor looks between us with this face like *I am a stone-cold killer.* "How was summer?"

"Good," we all say.

"Stay out of trouble?"

We nod.

Mr. Killroy looks at the notepad he's always carrying. "Hall Monitor, huh, Brock? That's good stuff. We need more leaders."

"To protect and serve is my only mission," Brock says. "Also, I'm in it for the free pretzels we get during Friday meetings."

"And Thomas: Saw you're going out for soccer. Outstanding."

"I probably won't make it," Tommy says.

"But you're trying." Mr. Killroy shifts his glare to me. "Derrick—what are you up to this year?"

I chew my pizza. Tommy and Brock make faces like *Uhhhhhh.*

But they're worried for zero reasons: No way I tell Killroy about my shed. Big giant dudes like him could body-slam a hole in the shelter and steal everything.

"Muscle mass," I say. "Operation Bulk Up."

"He's been pushing earth all summer," Brock says real quick. "He can do sixty-five pushups in two minutes."

"I can dig it," Mr. Killroy says. I think he flexes a little.

Then he hands me a little square piece of paper. It's a pass.

Please report to the guidance office at 1:20 p.m.

"Have a good first day, boys," he says, walking off.

3

At 1:15 p.m. I show the pass to my social studies teacher, Mr. Hines. He pulls on his big black beard with one hand. "I guess I'll see ya tomorrow."

I head to the front of the school and walk into the guidance office. The only good thing about this place is that it's air-conditioned.

"Hi, Derrick," says Mrs. Ruth, the guidance secretary. Actually, she's the other good thing about this place. Supernice and always brings in homemade cookies. "How was your summer?"

"Good."

Mr. Killroy comes out of his office. "Derrick. Come on in."

I follow him and sit in a chair next to his desk. Pictures of his kids and the basketball teams he's coached cover the walls. A big filing cabinet along the window has a couple trophies on it.

"So how's your first day going?" he asks.

"Good."

"Yeah? Tell me about it."

I shrug.

He nods.

"Last year I'd pull you in for a chat once in a while," Mr.

Killroy says. "I wanted to do the same this year. Your dad said that was okay."

"Okay."

"I know you don't like it."

"It's fine."

"How's Dr. Mike doing?"

"I don't know."

"You're not seeing him anymore?"

"No."

"How long has that been?"

I shrug.

Mr. Killroy waits a while. Feels like a minute. "Last year was rough. I know that."

I slouch and stare up at the tiled ceiling. There's a watermark right above me that sort of looks like that black knot of wood in the shed. The maintenance guy should really see if there's a leak there. "Uh-huh."

"I'm not a therapist," Mr. Killroy says. "But I've met with a lot of kids over the years sitting right in that chair—right where you're at. Some pretty hard things going on in their lives. I'm not saying you gotta come in here and tell me all about it, but if you need to talk, I'm here. You don't need a pass, just come on down."

I hear the click of the PLAY button in my head. The desert scene flashes for a couple seconds and then shuts off. "Yeah. I'm good."

Mr. Killroy nods. He swivels his chair and pulls a picture from his desk drawer. "Recognize this skinny punk?"

I take it. Looks like a school picture from eighty years ago. "No."

"That's me in eighth grade."

"Whoa." I see the face now, but it's weird without all the muscle.

"The kid in that picture had some issues. Anger, mostly, and it put him in worse places than the guidance office."

Prison? Maybe that's when he started lifting weights. "Hmm."

"You said you've been bulking up—you look bigger."

"Just pushups."

"Stuff like that helped me blow off steam too. A coach got me to try out for the football team, and it turned things around—having a place to put all my anger."

"I don't play sports," I say.

"That's fine." He hands me some kind of schedule. "My basketball players who aren't on the football team work out after school a couple times a week. Nothing crazy, just staying in shape for the season this winter. You don't have to be on the team to join them."

"Hmm."

"Think about it. You want to show up? Great. You can ride the sports bus home. It will definitely help you with your pushups. Maybe take your mind off some other stuff too."

"Okay." But not a chance because no time. And my mind is on exactly what it should be.

Mr. Killroy checks the clock on his wall and starts writing me a pass back to social studies. "And tell Mr. Hines to shave his beard. He looks like a fur trapper from the 1800s."

1

"It says online that stretching is supposed to hurt." Tommy is way down in a deep knee bend. "Which is good because, like, I'm in a lot of pain."

"Battery," I say.

He digs one out of my tool bag and gives it to me. "I think I pulled a muscle at practice today. It burns when I walk."

"What burns?"

"Everything."

"You should be eating lots of carbs," Brock yells. He's on the other side of Tommy's deck ripping out spindles. "Carb load."

"Kelly says carbs are bad," Tommy says. "It's over anyway. The roster is coming out Friday. I probably won't make it."

The back slider door of Tommy's deck opens and his mom comes out. "Boys—boys. Are you hydrating?"

"Yeah, Mom," Tommy says.

I point to my cooler filled with water bottles. Tommy's mom gives me that *Oh you poor thing* look that adults give me sometimes.

"Derrick—Derrick." She comes off her deck and puts a big, heavy arm around me. Tommy gets his close talking from her, probably. "Derrick—this is fabulous. You really know your deck repair. Everybody says so."

"Thanks."

"Just fantastic." Now she's got both arms wrapped around me. "How did you learn how to do all this?"

"See that grip," I hear Brock say to Tommy. "That's what Pete wants to do to you. All the time he thinks about doing this to you."

"Just learned it," I say. "From my dad."

"Right—right. Big construction manager." She pats me a bunch of times. "Just fantastic. How much do I owe you again?"

"I'll email you the invoice when we're done."

She laughs. "Invoice? So *mature*." She kisses the top of my head. Brock pretends his hands are the jaws of a snake and eats Tommy's entire head.

I put on the new spindles and Brock and Tommy stain them. We eat a snack of no carbs and then go up to Tommy's room and watch Pete doing nothing in his giant snake cage for a while. I push the earth fifty-six times in two minutes—not good. I'm tired from fixing Tommy's deck, which I'm only doing so I have extra cash in case I need to buy stuff last minute.

I'm at Tommy's computer doing the invoice when we hear this big *clunk* outside.

We go the window and see Misty in the middle of the

cul-de-sac, hauling a big cinder block out of her red wagon and putting it next to another one on the pavement. Now she's laying a big board on top like a ramp.

"This is going to be interesting," Brock says.

Misty straps on her helmet and gets on her bike. She's wearing all the pads you can wear—knee, elbow, wrist. Shin? I didn't know they made those. She rides out of view and then blazes back, heading right at the ramp. But she's sort of coming in crooked, so it rockets her to the left and she barely holds on for the landing.

"Oh man," I say. My stomach gets real tight. "That was close."

"Maybe we should, like, call someone," Tommy says.

"Who?" Brock asks.

"I don't know. Her mom. The police."

Misty rides around the jump a couple times. She stops to straighten the ramp out and then rides back out of view. This time she's going even faster at the jump and her face has this huge smile like *Oh man oh man this is going to be amazing.*

"Lean back," Brock says. "Lean back."

Misty hits the ramp straight on and flies a couple feet before her front tire slams down. It looks clean, but then the handlebars twist to the side, almost throwing her off. At the last second she leans the other way and saves herself a face-plant into a mailbox.

I throw open the window and yell, "You're using too much front brake."

Misty looks around and then sees us. Tommy waves real big like we're picking her up from the airport.

"Oh, hey." She waves back. "What did you say?"

"When you land," I shout. "Don't jam on the front brake. That's why you almost crashed."

"Okay. Cool."

Misty goes back to the jump and takes the board off. She stacks the two cinder blocks on top of each other so the ramp doubles in height.

"Guys," Tommy says. "I think we should really call someone."

I shout, "Don't do that."

"Why not?" Misty yells back.

"Why are you boys yelling?" Kelly screams from downstairs.

We wave Misty over and she pedals to grass.

"It's too steep," I say. "It'll collapse when you try to ride up. You could get really hurt."

"Huh." She tightens her elbow pads. "But I really need to get some air."

"You got some the first time," Brock says.

"Really? Both tires?"

"Yeah."

"You're sure?"

34

We all look at each other.

"Yeah," I say.

"Okay." Misty takes off a shoe and dumps some rocks out of it. "Hey, Derrick: You think I could borrow some tools?"

"For what?"

"This thing I'm doing."

"To build a bigger ramp?"

"No." She puts her shoe back on. "I'm done with the ramp."

"So what's it for?"

"I can't tell you until you say yes."

"Why not?"

She looks around, like people are listening. "It might be illegal."

"Hmm."

Misty shields her eyes from the sun. Man, she is really pale for the end of the summer. Vampire pale. "So, can you help me?" she asks.

"No," I say. Not a chance I risk getting arrested or her breaking my stuff. Not this close to The End. "Sorry."

"I'd let you borrow our stuff," Tommy says, "but Kelly doesn't let me have access to the garage."

"Who's Kelly?" Misty asks.

"His mom," Brock says. "She's kind of"—he mimes big giant claws—"mama bear."

"Oh yeah. I got one of those. That's why I'm doing all

this down here." Her phone dings and she checks it. "Derrick: We'll talk about those tools later."

She puts all the ramp stuff back in the wagon, and pulls it behind her as she walks her bike down the street.

"She's so weird," I say.

"Maybe she has a concussion," Tommy says. "From landing too hard."

"It's probably all the cancer drugs," Brock says.

"She didn't have cancer," I say.

"She had something," Tommy says. "She was out the whole year."

I nod because yeah, she was. Right?

Misty turns and waves before we lose sight of her. I think maybe she's looking at me, but it's hard to tell. I wave back and she smiles, and it's like the other night at my house—like we've done this before. Her pulling that red wagon, smiling and waving.

2

"**T**acos are ready!" Claudia shouts upstairs to my dad.

I'm in the living room pushing the earth and watching guys from Finland pull buses on ESPN3.

"Dinner!" Claudia yells again.

I slide up to the island bar and start building my taco. Probably this is the food I'm going to miss the most. My MREs only have a couple of flavors and the guys on *Apocalypse Soon!* say they all taste the same.

"We eat as a family," Claudia says.

I listen to my dad stomping around upstairs. "I'm hungry."

Claudia whips a dish towel at me as I take a bite—*snap.*

"Jeez!" I yell.

She's got a smirk on her face like *Go ahead, try it again.*

My dad finally comes down and sits on the other side of Claudia. He's dressed up and smells like cologne, which means he's meeting one of his Internet women tonight.

"How was work?" Claudia asks.

"Stuck in a township meeting most of the morning," he says. "Paperwork after that. Speaking of—Derrick. I got an interesting package today at the office."

I swallow a chunk of taco and almost choke. "What?"

"Gas masks. Five of them."

Crap. Default shipping on his credit card. Stupid mistake.

"They were supposed to come here," I say. "Where are they?"

"I gave him the card," Claudia says. "I didn't know he was going to get five of them."

"It's my money," I say.

"You should ask me next time," my dad says. "Or at least tell me."

"Why?" I pile meat on another taco. "So you can talk about it with one of your online girlfriends?"

Claudia kicks my barstool.

He waits a couple seconds and says, "You should tell me because I almost had the UPS guy take them back."

Claudia elbows me in the ribs. Gives me a face like *You're being a huge gigantic jerk.*

"Thanks for not sending them back," I say.

"They're in the garage. Just . . ." I see him lean forward and look down at me. I keep my eyes on the taco. "Just give me a heads-up next time."

"Uh-huh."

I devour three more tacos while Claudia updates us all on her "very rigorous AP courses" for this semester. I stare at the shed through the back slider, counting down the minutes until Claudia won't yell at me for leaving. I check my watch, give it two more, then rinse my plate and break for the garage.

3

I count the masks. All here. I put one in my go bag upstairs and haul the rest to the shed to stow in the bins.

I do my inventory, pretending I don't hear my dad's giant truck start up as he heads to his eHarmony meet-up. He'll probably tell her about my gas masks and she'll make a face like *Oh that poor, crazy boy* and then order a stupid fancy coffee drink that costs like ten bucks.

"Hey."

I look up and see Misty standing outside the door. She's got the red wagon with her. Empty. "Hey."

"How's it going?"

"Good."

She lets go of the wagon handle and walks up the little wooden ramp. Taps her foot on it. "So about those tools."

I shake my head. "I can't get arrested."

"Are you in witness protection or something?" She really needs to rub that sunblock in better. It's all caked on her eyebrows. "And if you get caught, the cops will run your fingerprints, and the mafia will come get you?"

"I need to finish this." I wave my hand at the shed. "For the apocalypse."

She doesn't blink or laugh or make a face like *You're crazy*. She just sort of stares. "Like, doomsday?"

"Yeah."

"When is it?"

"September twenty-first."

She frowns. "That really stinks."

"Yeah."

"That's my dad's birthday."

"Hmm."

"You're sure it's *this* September twenty-first?"

"Yeah."

"How do you know?"

"A total solar eclipse is aligning with the six-hundred-thousand-year anniversary of the eruption of the volcano under Yosemite National Park—which erupts every six hundred thousand years," I say. "There's other signs, like weather patterns around the world and stuff. But It's definitely happening."

"Huh."

She disappears. I hear her walking around the shed and go out to meet her.

"So what's gonna happen, when it blows?" she asks. "Can lava come this far?"

"No, but we'll be able to hear the explosion," I say. "Anybody within about a couple hundred miles will die pretty quickly. Ash clouds will mess with the atmosphere for years, wrecking farming in most of the country."

"My dad is gonna be majorly bummed when I tell him.

He really loves his birthday." She looks up at the sky and all around. "I mean, this is seriously not good."

"Yeah."

Misty looks at the shed. "Why are you covering up the wood with more wood?"

"Reinforce the walls."

"From what?"

"Weather and stuff. Mainly people trying to break in."

"What about the tree?" She looks up at the giant maple shading us. "What if it falls on the shed?"

"It's not gonna fall."

"I've seen tornadoes on TV that rip up trees pretty easily," she says. "Last time I was here, there was a couple big dead branches on the ground."

"It's fine," I say, but my brain goes *Last time? Last time?*

"But that's the kind of freak accident that would happen if it's the end of the world, right?"

Last time? "It's not gonna fall."

Misty bangs on the plywood. "Okay, but if someone had an ax, they could probably chop right through this. Or light it on fire. Why didn't you just build a new one with cinder blocks?"

"You're not allowed to build something like that here," I say. "I tried, but the property deed says you can't."

Misty walks around the whole shed again. "Not very big. Gonna be crammed."

"It's just for me."

"What about your dad and Claudia?"

"They don't think It's happening."

"What if they change their minds?"

I shrug. "They can live in the house."

"Huh."

We both sort of watch the shed together. Now I'm looking at her and she's looking at me and it's really awkward, so I say, "You were gone most of last year."

"Yeah."

"You were . . . sick." I say it real slow. "That's why you missed lots of school."

Misty watches me. Nods again.

"Hmm."

"Derrick—" she says, but stops. Shrugs it off.

My stomach knots and I say, "Where'd you get that wagon?"

"What?"

I point at it. "Is that like—did you borrow that from me a while ago?"

Misty squints at me real hard. *"What?"*

"Never mind."

The sun goes below the houses. Misty takes off her Phillies hat and says, "So about those tools."

"Yeah. No."

"Okay." She sighs. "See ya."

She crosses the Mitchells' yard to her deck that needs like a million repairs and leaves the wagon at the steps. After she goes inside I walk around the shed and give the wall a bang with my fist. It's solid, right? Right. It is. It has to be, because I can't lay cinder block. I'm not allowed. And what does Misty know about The End? She's not a member of the best doomsday blog on the Internet. She doesn't know anything about tornadoes or falling trees or exploding underground volcanoes.

The back floodlight on her house switches on. Probably on a timer or something. I can see the tracks her wagon made in the grass from her house, across the Mitchells', right to the shed.

Maybe it's mine. Did she steal it?

1

The fridge lights up the kitchen like one of those police helicopter beams. I dig around until I find the leftover taco meat and microwave it. I crumble some chips on top and shovel it down in the dark. The stove clock says 12:22. I've been up late watching YouTube videos of guys ramming stuff into plywood to make sure I'll be safe in the shed if somebody tried that.

There's some mail on the kitchen table and I move it to the island. We haven't used that table since It happened. Claudia tried to set dinner there one time and I lost it, lots of screaming and stuff. Apparently I cried. I don't really remember it all, but I remember totally freaking out. Around then, my dad started making me go talk to Dr. Mike.

Probably it was my dad who put that mail there. He probably sits there when we go to bed, emailing his Internet girlfriends on his laptop. I kind of want to flip the table over right now.

Bang.

I freeze.

Was that from the garage?

Bang.

I sneak through the laundry room and put my ear to the door. Nothing for a while.

Bang.

It's like someone is trying to break into the garage. Should I call the police? Maybe wake up my dad—but no. My tools. Whoever is trying to bust in could steal them and then I won't be able to put the steel door on my shed, which would ruin everything. That buzzing is halfway up my arms.

I go out the back slider door that leads to the deck and bolt for the shed. I dig this big heavy police Maglite flashlight from one of my bins and sprint to the side of the house, peeking around the corner. There's a shadow crouched by the garage, small and hunched over a light. I tiptoe, still barefoot, heart pounding, ready to flick the switch and yell *GET THE CRAP AWAY* when I smell sunscreen.

And see that the light is really a phone screen.

Playing a YouTube video.

I can hear it too: A guy is talking about garage doors. The small shadow sets it down and starts messing with the lock.

"Hey," I say.

"AH!" Misty yells, falling over. Her phone skitters on the driveway and must've hit a button, because now a commercial is playing. Some lady is talking about a new show or something with lots of dancing. Misty dives for the phone and rolls onto the grass, laughing. She's covering her mouth and saying "I'm sorry, I'm sorry."

"I thought you were a robber," I whisper.

Misty nods but still can't pull it together. "I'm the worst robber ever."

"Yeah. You are."

"So what's the garage code?"

"You're not getting in the garage."

"Oh right—we should use the back slider door," she says, walking around to the side of the house toward the deck. "That way we don't wake anybody up."

I jog after her. "What are you doing?"

"You kept saying no."

"So you were going to steal from me?"

"Borrow," she says, leaping up my deck steps. "Like before. It's what neighbors do."

Before.

I beat her to the back slider and say, "I don't even—Misty. You've never done this before."

"Yes, I have—and you never said no." She gives me a face like *Are you serious right now?* "Now: Do you want in on my adventure or not?"

Our kitchen light goes on and I duck behind the grill. "Get down."

Misty knocks on the glass and waves.

The door opens and Claudia says, "Are you okay?"

"Oh—yeah. I'm fine." Misty points at my hiding spot. "Derrick said I could borrow some tools."

"Oh," Claudia says, and she sounds all relieved. "Wait—he did?"

"Okay, not really true. I tried to break into the garage using this YouTube video. Bad idea. It led to my capture."

"I didn't capture you," I say, ditching my hiding spot.

Claudia lets us in and does a lot of yawning and eye rubbing and then goes back up to bed. Misty marches to the garage like she owns the place and stares at the workbench with all the tools and stuff hanging on a giant pegboard above it. "This is intense."

"What do you even need?"

Misty grabs one of my dad's big drills. "Whoa."

"You need *that*?"

"No, it's just pretty cool." She puts it down and starts opening plastic containers where I keep screws and bolts. "I need a key."

"A what?"

"The guy on YouTube called it a key. But not like a door key."

"Hmm," I say. "Like a painter's key?"

"Not sure."

Ugh.

I go over to the shelf where my dad keeps all the paint supplies and dig out a painter's key. It's a four-inch piece of metal that has a tiny hook on the end that pries open paint can lids. "Did it look like this?"

Misty takes it from me and starts trying to pry up random stuff on the workbench. "How much weight can this hold?"

I shrug. "Probably not much."

"Okay." She hands it back and says, "Then I'm gonna need a crowbar."

"Oh jeez," I say. "No way."

"Why don't you just help me?"

"Could one of us get hurt?"

Misty thinks about that. "Probably not."

"This is all not good," I say, and try to beat her to the big crowbar hanging on the pegboard, but she's too fast and snatches it. I try to grab it, but she pulls it away and almost hits me in the face with the hook end and I say, "What are you gonna do with that?"

"Okay, okay, okay: You know those big metal circles in the road? The metal things that lead to the sewers."

"Manhole covers?"

"I want to pop one open and see what's down there."

I watch her face to see if she's kidding.

Not kidding.

"Why?"

Misty smiles real wide. "You're not curious what's down there?"

"I know what's down there. Poop."

"Like, flowing by?"

"I don't know. Probably."

"You said you knew."

"Everybody knows what's down there. They're sewer tunnels. Poop goes into the sewers."

"I want to see it for myself." Misty moves the crowbar between her hands and almost drops it. "I want to pry it off, slide it over, and look down."

"But, like—*why?*"

Misty's face gets all serious. "Because I want to. So are you in or what?"

"No."

"Your loss."

"Just don't drop my crowbar into a bunch of poop, okay? I need it."

We go back in the house and Misty heads for the front door. Just walks right out to the street. The moon is pretty bright, so I can see her standing over the manhole cover right near my driveway, her phone light on. How the heck is she even gonna pry it off? It probably weighs more than her. A neighbor is gonna hear the noise and see her and probably call the police. And then I'll get busted too as an accomplice or something because I gave her the crowbar.

Also, she could get run over, which would be so lame since she just got back from being sick.

Ugh.

I run up to my room, grab my headlamp from the go bag, and race back down and out the front door.

"AH!" she yells when I sneak up on her. "Stop doing that."

"Do you know how to actually do this?"

She thinks for a second. "The YouTube guy said you put the hook end in the hole, twist it, and then just pry it off." She does it and pulls back really hard.

Not budging.

I grab it with her and we're leaning way back now and the cover lifts up an inch but my grip slips and the whole thing slams down with a gigantic *bangclang!* Misty chokes on a laugh and I switch off my headlamp. We look around.

No lights on.

"Come on," she says. *"Come on!"*

I switch my lamp back on and we reset the crowbar and lean with our whole bodies. This time it comes up farther and then all of a sudden we're falling back as the whole thing slides off.

Misty crawls over and shines her phone down the gap. "Wow," she whispers.

I look around. A light down the street is on. Another one pops on, closer. "We gotta go."

"Come look."

I peek down and see a ladder that goes about ten feet

into some water flowing by. There's some bigger pipes but not much else.

"So where's the poop?" she asks.

"Maybe this isn't the poop tunnel." Then real quick I say, "We're not going down there."

"I know. But it would be cool if we did."

"Seriously, we need to go."

"Okay."

We try to push the cover back into place with our feet. It's harder than getting it off because it won't just sit any way—it has to be perfectly over the hole. And it's really heavy. I try to shove it with the crowbar, but that makes a big, loud *bangclang*.

"Crap!" I whisper. More lights pop on—one right across the street. *"Oh man."*

"Come on!" Misty says, but there's a laugh behind it as she kicks at it. *"Come on!"*

"I'm trying."

"Hey!" somebody yells down the street, just as the cover sinks into place. We scramble up and I grab the crowbar and a guy yells *"Stop!"* but there's no way that's happening. We pound down the pavement, away from our houses. We're fear sprinting like those gazelles on a safari, bounding over bushes and around trees in total panic. We keep running until our lungs give out two streets away and then cut back through a couple yards to my shed. Inside Misty collapses

on the cot and does this laugh that sounds like a choking donkey.

"Oh man," I say. "Oh *man.*"

She keeps laughing, rolling and building as she works up to a huge *"Whaaaaaaaaaaaaaaaaaat!"* that echoes off the shed walls.

1

"So I ask the kid for his hall pass," Brock says. "And he tells me that Mrs. Mason didn't give him one."

Tommy is staring at his phone, refreshing it every five seconds. I'm inhaling everybody's tater tots because I didn't eat yesterday—too busy sleeping after Misty almost got me arrested. My dad wanted to take me to the doctor, but I made something up and just lay in bed all day.

"Which is hilarious," Brock says, "because Mrs. Mason would never let a seventh grader out of her room without a pass. She has records of every kid who left her room going back decades. That is the truth."

"Guys," Tommy says. He shakes his head. "I'm not going to make the team."

"I thought you wanted to get cut," I say.

"I did before." He eats his nails. "But, like, now it's fun. And Kelly said if I don't make the team, I have to go to the YMCA. It smells like bleach and everybody has big calves."

Brock pulls his tray away from me. "What's your situation?"

"I'm starving." I look over and see Misty at a table with some other girls. They're talking and looking at stuff on their phones. She's reading. Probably a book about sewers.

"Come on," Tommy says to his phone.

"Dee, you keep staring at Misty," Brock asks. "Do you like her?"

"What?" My face gets hot and I stop eating. "No. No."

"You said no, like, pretty fast," Tommy says.

"I'm not. She's—" Tommy's eyebrows are going up and down like *Hey, hey, hey*. "Okay. Okay. Listen."

I tell them about Operation Manhole Cover. By the end, Tommy forgets he even has a phone. Brock's shaking his head, smiling.

"Whoa," Tommy says. "She's, like, way, way off."

"I know. Right?"

"She's awesome," Brock says.

"What?"

"She threw that hatchet until she hit a bull's-eye," he says. "And then, boom, she's on to the next thing. Midnight robbery and looking down manholes. She's unstoppable." He slides his tray back so I can have the last of his tots. "She's crushing life."

"We could've gotten arrested," I say. "Or run over. Or maybe put the cover on wrong and a car crashed because of us."

"Maybe."

"Guys," Tommy says. His phone is an inch from his face. "Guys."

"*Yes!*" some kid at another table yells. He's on his phone too, showing it to the guys around him.

"You guys." Tommy leans in and says real low, "I made it."

Brock lets out a whoop and smacks the table. He stands up and shouts, "Ladies and gentlemen: Witness the newest member of the Kennesaw Middle School eighth-grade soccer team."

Tommy looks like he won the lottery.

"Would you like to say a few words?" Brock asks, sticking his fist in front of Tommy like a fake microphone. "Something to let us know how you overcame the odds and made this possible."

Tommy is just laughing and in shock.

"Good job, dude," I say.

"Thanks. Maybe, like, you guys can come to my game or something."

"Oh, we're coming," Brock says. "Starting with practice today."

Mr. Killroy announces that it's time to clean up. I can see Tommy eyeing me. I wait a couple seconds and then say, "Yeah. Yeah, we'll be there," even though the soccer field is a mosquito playground and I have a million things to do for the shed still.

"Cool." Tommy bumps into me as we're dumping our trays. I want to elbow him out of my space really hard. "Cool."

2

Tommy sprints down the sideline and catches up with the kid who has the ball. He forces him to the outside, and then blocks the ball as the kid tries to kick it.

"He's really fast," I say. "Like a rabbit."

"He might be the fastest person here," Brock says.

Brock holds up the sign he just made during Resource, this study hall we get at the end of the day.

TOMMY EATS ONLY BEEF AND YOUR TEARS it says.

"Maybe everybody else is just really slow," I say.

A dad turns around and gives us a face like *That's rude.*

"Kelly is loving this," Brock says. We watch Tommy's mom follow him up and down the sideline with water bottles in each hand. Tommy runs a circle around another kid with the ball.

"Hey." Misty plops down next to me on the bleachers. Smells like the beach. "I have a present for you."

She digs into her backpack and hands me a picture of a doomsday bunker.

"This is the Underground ArkMini—the best bomb shelter on the planet. It's got everything: kitchen, toilet, water pressure pump, and a solar-generated charging system. Best part is, it's underground, so it's not really another structure."

"Yeah." I already know the specs because anybody who knows anything about The End knows about the ArkMini. "Thanks."

"You should get this."

"It costs forty thousand dollars. Plus the money to dig the big giant hole to put it in."

"Isn't your dad in construction? He could do it."

I stick it in my pocket. "I've got a shelter."

She shrugs. We watch soccer for a while. Brock whacks a hornet with his binder.

"Can I get a ride home with you guys?" Misty asks. "I had bass cello lessons, but they're over and my sister has swim practice until six."

"Kelly is taking us home," I say. "We can ask her after practice, I guess."

"Cool."

A kid is winding up for a shot on goal when Tommy streaks in and boots the ball out of bounds.

"He's fast," Misty says.

"He might have jet fuel for blood." Brock waves his sign.

"That's funny," she says. "I got one—here."

Misty grabs the sign and flips it over. She pulls a Sharpie from her pocket—who carries a Sharpie?—and writes TOMMY'S DINER: NOW SERVING SPEED AND HUMILIATION.

"Because he's so fast," she says. "And his speed humiliates his opponents."

"Boom," Brock says.

Misty gives him the sign back. "I really wanted to try out for the team, but my doctor said I can't."

I say, "Why?" and Brock says, "Because of the cancer," and then we're both staring at the field waiting for her to say something.

"'Cause of my kidney," Misty says. "I got a transplant in June, so I can't play contact sports for a while. Plus I'm not supposed to be in the sun that much. I'm on these medicines that make it really bad for my skin."

Kidney.

Transplant.

"Right," I say. "Yeah."

"I'm totally fine and everything," she says. "I mean, I almost died, but now I'm good."

"That would make a great sign," Brock says. "For people to carry around hospitals and cheer sick people on to get better."

Misty does her choking donkey thing. Brock sort of grunts out a laugh. I look between them wondering how almost dying is funny. My fingers buzz a little and my palms feel kinda wet, so I rub them on my shorts really hard.

Kidney.

Transplant.

The soccer coach blows his whistle to end practice.

Tommy weasels out of Kelly's mama bear hug and walks over to us.

"Witness me, like, not being totally bad," he says.

Brock high-fives him and shows him the sign Misty made. "Because you're fast and force-feed people lots of humiliation."

A soccer ball trickles over from the field. Misty runs at it full speed and boots it really hard but really awkwardly. It goes flying off at a side angle I don't think she was aiming for. She's grinning. She doesn't care.

"You know girls can play on the boys team," Tommy says. "If, like, they're playing another sport in the spring when the girls play."

"She can't," Brock says. "She almost died. But now she's fine."

Tommy leans real close to Misty and says, "The cancer."

"No," Misty says. "*Kid-ney*. And I'm totally fine."

"Like, for good?"

"Yup."

"'Cause Kelly rented this movie where the kid got better but then he got sick again," Tommy says. "Kelly was crying."

"Just Kelly?" Brock asks.

"It's not like that," Misty says. "Literally impossible for it to come back." She spots another ball on the sideline way down and rushes at it like a freight train, pulverizing it with her foot. It goes a little more straight.

"Crushing life," Brock says.

"Why weren't we friends with her before?" Tommy says. "She's, like, the coolest person ever."

"Hmm," I say.

Before.

1

eep-beep-beep goes the alarm on my watch.

I launch upright and jam my feet into my shoes in one motion—super-clean.

I throw the gas mask on and cinch the strap tight—perfect seal.

I throw my go bag on and sprint out of my bedroom and down the hallway. Claudia is probably snoring and I might wake her up, but too bad. She should thank me, actually. Sleeping in this close to The Big Day is like swimming in a gator swamp.

I fly down the steps three at a time and barrel out the back slider. I'm at the shed in twenty steps, opening the doors, and slamming them behind me. I hit the STOP button on my watch and rip the mask off to check the time.

Thirty-two seconds.

New record.

I open the shed doors to let some air in. It's only six thirty, but already super-humid. I really hope summer decides to get out of here in the next two weeks, or the shed is gonna be a sauna.

I practice the whole escape plan three more times and then drink a gallon of water. I inventory all my supplies, rearrange my medical kit so I can get to the bandages easier, and then push the earth until I'm all sweaty again. I stink pretty bad, so I take a shower and head to the garage to make sure all my drill batteries are charged for when the steel door gets here.

My dad pops his head inside. "Wanna go to the driving range and hit some golf balls?"

"Nah."

"Batting cages are right there too," he says. "Could do those."

"I'm good."

He stands for a couple seconds. "You sure?"

"Yeah."

"I can wait till you're done."

My phone buzzes and it's Tommy saying *I'm feeding Pete tomorrow come over.* "It's fine."

He goes away.

I put the drills away and open the garage doors. Claudia never checks her tires, which is stupid because a blowout might send you into a ditch or into another car. I roll the air compressor out and do it for her, then go inside and make a giant turkey sandwich.

"Thought you were going to hit golf balls," Claudia says. She's at the island taking notes from a giant textbook.

"Nah."

"Would it kill you to do something with him?"

"Yeah," I say. "It might, actually."

I pile the turkey so high it's ridiculous. Maybe this is the best sandwich ever, I'm not sure. Maybe I'm just so pumped to have gotten my time down to thirty-two seconds. Maybe I'm still coming out of that sleep hibernation.

"So what happened with Misty the other night?" Claudia asks.

"She wanted to take off a manhole cover. To see what was underneath."

"Did you?"

"Yeah."

"I love that girl."

"Ugh." I grab a Gatorade and wash down a huge chunk of turkey. "What's even her deal, anyway?"

Claudia doesn't answer, just keeps taking notes. I think about Misty saying *kidney transplant.*

"She was sick," I say. "How bad was it? Was it bad?"

Claudia looks up at me like *Really?*

I look at my sandwich and chew for a while. My brain is whirling like crazy on *kidney transplant,* but I got nothing. "Just tell me. Jeez."

"It was pretty serious," she says. "I forget the name of it—FSG something. She was in the hospital most of last year until the transplant."

That makes sense. I don't remember seeing her in school. "When did it all start?"

"October," Claudia says. "Right after."

After.

I'm watching her real close, wondering if that's the end of her sentence. She stares back and says, "Derrick: You're freaking me out."

"Gotta check on something," I say, and get the heck out of there.

2

n my room, I email the company I bought the steel door from to see what the crap is going on. They send me this message that they'll respond within two days, which is what they said when I emailed them last week, and they never did. I look at the big calendar above my desk and count backward from The End trying to figure out when is the last possible day the door could come and I'd still have time to install it. My room feels really hot, so I stand right under the AC vent and make fists, trying to get rid of that buzzing.

"Dee," Claudia calls up the steps. "Misty's here."

"Why?"

"I don't know."

I go downstairs and meet her on the deck.

"Do you have a net?" she asks.

"What kind of net?"

"Any kind. Fishing or butterfly net."

"I don't think so."

"Huh," she says. "Could you make one out of something? With a really long handle?"

"I don't know. Probably. For what?"

"To catch a bird."

"What bird?"

"Don't worry about it," she says. "Just will you make it or not?"

"I can't right now."

"Why not?"

"I'm busy."

Misty eye-rolls. "You're probably playing video games."

"I don't play video games. They're dumb."

"Then what are you doing?"

"None of your business."

She folds her arms. "You used to be way nicer to me."

"What?"

"When I'd come over to borrow stuff. You weren't like this. You'd say something funny and then we'd go find what I needed. Sometimes we ate Cheez-Its."

My eyes are going back and forth real fast and my stomach cramps. *When I'd come over.* "Stop saying stuff like that."

"What?"

"You didn't—listen." I think I'm sweating. Misty squints real hard at me like *What is happening with you* and I grab the door frame. "I'm just busy," I say. "Sorry."

"I'll pay you." She does some math in her head. "I've got some chore money I was saving for something, but this is kind of an emergency."

Now I feel like a jerk. "You don't have to pay me."

"So you'll do it?"

I blow out a long sigh. "Yeah."

"Awesome. Bring it over when you're done, but come to the front door—*not* the back. Okay? But don't ring the doorbell."

"Why not?"

But she's already sprinting across the Mitchells' yard to her house.

I go to the garage and pull down a couple of old bins. Most are packed with kid toys, but one of them has a bunch of old fishing stuff. I pull out a net that stinks like rotten ocean and bring it over to the workbench. I find a painting rod and duct-tape the net handle to it like an extension.

"Just in time," Misty says after I knock on her front door. She grabs the net stick thing and swings it around. "Sweet."

"Ahhhh!" somebody screams from inside. There's a blur in the air, and then her sister sprints across the living room and screams again.

"What was that?" I ask.

"Brynn really hates birds."

"Why is there a bird flying around in your house?"

"She's a homing pigeon," Misty says, marching toward the living room. I follow. "Her name is Pigeon."

"Her name is *dead*," Brynn shrieks. She's crouching in the kitchen with a binder over her head.

"She's just a little confused," Misty says. "It's her first mission."

I see a gray-and-white bird dive-bomb Brynn. She yells

and drops to the floor just as the thing pulls up and perches on an open cabinet door. Misty creeps toward Pigeon with the net and slowly raises it up. Pigeon cocks her head and then takes off back to the ceiling fan way up in the living room.

"Mom and Dad are going to *kill* you," Brynn yells. "She's already pooped on the couch."

I back against the wall so I don't get pooped on. "Why did you let her out?"

"It's part of her training," Misty says. She's digging in the fridge now for something, and comes out with a piece of bread. "You establish their home base—that's her cage in my room. Then you take them away and they fly back to their home. You can do it up to a hundred miles."

"Maybe her radar is off or something," I say.

"You think?" Brynn says. She starts crawling toward the stairs. Pigeon dives like a daredevil pilot, buzzing the wall and sending Brynn scrambling back to the kitchen. *"Misty! Seriously!"*

"Just stop moving!" Misty yells. She's smirking. She thinks this is hilarious. "It's probably all that hair stuff you use."

"Just do something."

"Okay, okay!"

"Put the bread in the net," I say. "Maybe she'll fly into it."

Misty drops a couple crumbs in and then holds the net up real high.

Pigeon fluffs her tail. Some white stuff drops on the carpet.

"Hmm," I say.

Misty lowers the net and takes the bread out. She looks at Brynn, then Pigeon, then the net. Back at Brynn, who's got her binder on her head like a helmet.

"No," I say.

"What?" Brynn asks.

"Uh," I say, but Misty gives me a face like *Shut up, shut up* and then she's putting some bread on top of the binder.

"What are you doing?" Brynn whispers, but she's like fear frozen and can't move.

Pigeon flutters off the fan, does a couple swoops past the fireplace before landing on the binder. She pecks for one second before Brynn shrieks and then *whamp*—Misty slams the net over it.

"Grab it, Derrick!" she shouts, and I race over to hold the binder. Brynn scrambles out from under it as Misty and I rotate the net, cinching it so there's no way out.

"Bad Pigeon." Misty holds her up so their eyes are level. "Bad girl."

"I cannot believe you just trapped a pigeon on my head," Brynn yells from the stairs. "You are so cleaning up all the poop." Some doors slam and then I hear water running through the pipes.

"What now?" I ask.

"Back to home base."

I follow her upstairs. She stops outside her room and says, "You can't come in."

"Okay."

Misty opens the door a tiny bit and tries to squeeze through, but the net and pole thing get stuck. She has to open it a little wider, and for a second I see inside. It's not that messy, so I don't know what she's being weird about— some clothes and paper on the floor. Actually, not paper, index cards, all sort of lined up. She slams the door shut before I can see any more.

In a minute she comes back with the net. "Thanks."

"Yeah."

We have a stare-off and then she says, "This is what it was like."

"What?"

"Before."

I can feel my brain trying to click.

"I gotta go," I say, and head back down the steps. "See ya."

At home, I scrub my hands with bleach and then shower in case Pigeon has bird flu. That would not be a good thing to catch this close to The End.

"**P**opcorn is ready," Claudia says.

"Uh-huh."

She hangs outside my room. "Brock and Tommy are here."

I scroll to the *Apocalypse Soon!* weather alerts. Some weird stuff is hitting Australia and there's all this chatter about a tsunami. "I'm just gonna stay up here."

"Dee: Movie roulette is sacred."

"I don't feel like it."

"It's the one tradition we still do."

That desert movie flicks on in my brain. It's on fast-forward or something and gets farther this time. I see the giant dust cloud way at the end of the road. A couple Humvees burst out of it and come speeding at me and the ground rumbles and I have to work really hard to shut it off.

"Maybe I don't want to anymore."

Claudia comes in my room. She puts her hand on my forehead and says, "You're sweating."

I swat her hand away. "I'm fine."

She looks at the giant calendar hanging above the desk for a while and then grabs a marker and draws a little heart on Thursday, September 13. Five days from now. Eight days before The End.

I stare back at my computer.

"Do it for me," she says. "Eat Dad's awesome popcorn and watch something probably stupid for two hours because *I* want you to."

I look at the heart, then back down. Ugh. "Fine."

I wait till she's gone before scribbling out the stupid heart.

Downstairs I dig through a big collection of DVDs in the family room and pick a zombie one because there's always useful survival stuff in those. In the kitchen Brock is pouring giant cups of Mountain Dew Code Red and I get one.

"Kelly says butter is bad," Tommy is telling my dad. "She says you might as well, like, shove a stick of dynamite into your heart."

"What does she think about salt?" my dad asks him.

Tommy gives a thumbs-down. He chews on the weird trail mix he brought.

"That smells like mulch," Brock says, taking a whiff of the bag.

"Okay, people," Claudia says. "Put your cards on the table."

We all lay our DVD choices on the island counter. Claudia won last time, so she gets to put down two. Seven options total.

"Again with the LEGO movie," Brock says to Tommy.

Claudia swipes it off the counter. "Sorry, dude."

Brock pulls my zombie movie next. Tommy gets rid of Claudia's live-action musical and my dad takes out her other one, some lame romance movie. I'm last to go. Easy: the stupid Western from like fifty years ago my dad loves.

Brock's action movie is the only one left.

"Boom," he says. "You can thank my dad. He just bought it today."

"I heard it was good," my dad says.

Claudia puts the movie in and my dad hits the lights. I lie on the floor with a big pillow and eat the world's saltiest popcorn. The plot gets going and Brock and Tommy make bets on which character is going to die first. I'm actually sort of glad Claudia forced me down here. It's kind of a break from thinking about The End.

"Watch this," my dad says, and then everybody laughs as the secret agent guy punches right through a steel door. I'm laughing too and it feels really good. I think my ribs might actually split when Tommy makes Claudia rewind it and we watch it again in slow motion.

My popcorn's gone, so I get up to wash my hands. I'm rinsing them in the sink when I see my dad check his phone. He types something real quick and I wonder what he would be texting his construction guys this late on a Saturday.

And then what he said echoes in my head—*watch this*. That's a weird thing to say. How would you know something totally hilarious was about to happen in a movie that just came out? Isn't that what Brock said? That his dad just bought it? Today?

Watch this.

So he's already seen it.

I heard this was good.

And he's lying about it.

"Earth to Dee," Brock says, behind me at the sink.

I know why he lied. It's the same reason he gets all dressed up and goes out after dinner.

He took one of his Internet women to see this movie.

In the theater.

On a date.

Now they're texting about it, really laughing it up about what a great time they had and I'm watching him here and now the room is sort of tilting.

I go upstairs and slam my door. Lock it. I'm shaking and my fists are clenching and unclenching and I'm walking back and forth and then Tommy is outside saying *Dee, are you okay?* But I don't answer. I just keep walking back and forth and back and forth and I want to scream or cry or throw something and it's like a hundred degrees in here and I'm sweating pretty bad now.

I push the earth. The desert movie plays again, but after around sixty pushups I'm too tired and it shuts off. My muscles burn, but I actually feel less hot. I lie on the carpet and see Tommy's shadow outside my room, sitting on the floor.

I don't know how long he stays, but he's there when I fall asleep.

1

I wake up angry.

My watch says *10:30 a.m.*, which turns the rage dial up even more.

I overslept. Not a good survival habit.

I hurry to the bathroom and brush my teeth. Popcorn stuck everywhere. I guzzle a ton of water and then go back to my room and look at the calendar.

Twelve days.

Pretty bad time to get lazy.

I check for updates on *Apocalypse Soon!* and go downstairs. The kitchen is empty, so I eat cereal and watch Romanian guys carry sandbags from one side of a gym to the other on TV. Claudia comes back in from a jog and glares at me. Then she pretends I'm not there.

"I didn't feel good," I say.

"I get it, Dee. *Anything* that reminds you of Mom is totally off-limits. Message received. No more movie nights." Claudia rips her earbuds out and tosses them on the counter. "Maybe we should just move. Maybe we should change our last name."

"No, that's not why—"

"Everybody wants you to get better," she says. "Don't

you get it? We're all rooting for you. But it's like you don't even want to. You're okay being this way."

This way. I shake my head. "You don't get it."

"Whatever."

I go out to the shed and push the earth until I'm drenched. *Get better.* Like I'm the crazy person here who thinks our dad shouldn't be going on Internet dates and seeing spy movies and then texting about it in our house. During movie night—a tradition *She* started.

"Knock knock."

Misty's standing there in her normal getup: shorts, T-shirt, Phillies hat. Sunscreen so thick, she's a ghost.

"I was thinking," she says. "You might want to have this tree trimmed before the apocalypse. Because there's a couple dead limbs and they might fall, and you're not going to want to do that kind of work when the world is ending."

"What's your problem?" I ask. It echoes off the walls pretty good, so I must've yelled. "What are you even doing here?"

Misty walks away.

Then she comes back, with some water she just took from my cooler. "You're probably really dehydrated. It can make people angry."

I walk outside and sit in the shade. It feels twenty degrees cooler. I chug the water. Maybe I am dehydrated.

Misty pulls the cooler over to me and sits on it. "Don't you think people are too polite?"

"What?"

"They never say what they should. They just say what's polite. Which is stupid because if you were sitting on a train track, and a train was coming, I wouldn't ask you in this nice way to get off. I'd scream."

I shrug.

She picks a dandelion from the grass and flings it. "I used to hate talking in front of people. In fourth grade, I peed myself during a class presentation on George Washington."

"Why are you telling me this?"

Misty takes off her Phillies hat and puts her face in some sunlight breaking through the leaves. Maybe she's like a reverse vampire: She comes alive under UV rays.

"In the movies, when somebody young finds out they're dying, they're sad about missing out on true love and stuff." Misty shakes her head. "I mean—true love is probably cool, but there's a million more things. A billion more. A billion billion."

"Mmhm."

"They all pile up, and it just gets higher." She's doing that really serious face again—the Misty Stare. Her eyes are hard, like what you'd find if you drilled down to the center of a piece of steel. "But I got better. So now I get to do them. And one of those things is saying what I want and not caring what people think."

I swat a mosquito on my neck and miss. Brock would be ashamed of me. "Okay."

"Do you get it?"

The mosquito goes after my arm and I get it this time. I think about keeping it in case I get sick, to maybe analyze it for West Nile. "You're trying to cram it all in or something. Because life is short."

"More like: Life is a buffet. And it's gonna close at some point. So eat up." The Stare fades a little. "Like the Brazilian one by the old air base with all the meat platters. I really want to go there for my birthday."

"Brock went there for his cousin's graduation. He ate so much he barfed most of the next day."

Misty does her choking donkey laugh. Her smile is that giant one again—like this is the funniest moment of her life. "Classic."

I drink some more water and think about what she just said. "The food won't taste good," I say. "The closer you get to the buffet shutting down, you'll start to hate it. You'll just be thinking about how it's going to close and then it will all taste like gruel pouches."

"What're gruel pouches?"

"This thing Tommy's mom makes," I say. "Fruits and vegetables all ground together and shoved into these pouches."

"He eats those?"

"He used to," I say. "He says he doesn't anymore but I've seen 'em in his fridge."

Misty shrugs. "Maybe you're right. But I just got to the buffet and it all looks amazing. I don't see any gruel pouches."

"Okay." I shrug. "So what's next?"

"It was the bass cello, but I decided to quit. Too boring. Really hard to carry around."

"Hmm."

"That's actually why I'm here."

"What?"

"*Mercedes,*" her mom shouts. "We're leaving."

Misty puts her Phillies hat back on. "Swim meet. Gotta support the sister." She jogs out of the shed and calls over her shoulder, "To be continued."

2

"**M**aybe he's not hungry," Tommy says.

A white mouse walks right by Pete's tail. This mouse has guts or is totally stupid.

"When did you feed him last?" I ask.

"A week ago. Maybe he's, like, sick."

"Maybe he's saving up," Brock says. He gets real close to Tommy and breathes on his face. "For the main course."

Tommy shoves him and then there's this blur as the mouse runs right by Pete's nose. He stops an inch away and just sits there, nibbling something.

"Oh man," I say. "He's almost dead and doesn't even—"

Snap!

We all scream as Pete bites the mouse and then strangles it in his giant body.

Then he swallows the entire thing.

"I guess he's okay," Tommy says.

Kelly comes in and says, "Thomas: I just got off the phone with Uncle Leo. He and Aunt Deloris are coming to your game this week."

"It's just a scrimmage," he says, but he's smiling real wide. "I might not even play that much."

"They're coming." She straightens a picture frame on

the wall that I'm pretty sure was already straight and then leaves.

"I will heckle the coach if he tries to take you out," Brock says. He grabs an Xbox controller and unpauses the FIFA game he and Tommy were playing. Kelly got it so Tommy could work on his soccer strategy. "I will tell him that you have a ball python developing a taste for people, and that we're not afraid to use it."

My phone buzzes. I check it and see a UPS shipping alert. *Your package will be delivered Tuesday.*

Oh.

Man.

The steel door.

It's coming.

This is amazing.

"What day is the scrimmage?" I ask.

"Tuesday," Tommy says.

Crap.

"What's wrong?"

"That steel door I ordered is coming Tuesday. I need to be there for it."

"Can't they just leave it there?" Brock asks.

"Yeah, but I need to check it and stuff. Make sure it's not damaged." Mostly I want to put it on right away.

Tommy bites his nail and says, "Yeah yeah yeah, it's fine."

"Maybe the next one."

"Cool. Yeah." He goes down the hall to the bathroom.

Brock gives me a flat face like *Dude, come on.*

"I have to be there," I say.

"Yeah." He dribbles his guy down the field and crushes the ball past Tommy's goalie. "You said that."

3

Kelly makes dinner, so Brock and I leave because her food makes our insides hurt. We ride our bikes side by side but don't say anything except "See ya" when he peels off to his street. I don't really have anything to do right now on the shed, so I just ride around. The air feels kind of nice going this fast.

"Hey," Misty yells, pedaling up behind me. Got all the pads on again, shin ones too. "Where you going?"

"Just riding."

She catches up with me, so I guess we're riding together now. We cut down a dirt path that goes behind our neighborhood into this tiny patch of woods. It's pretty twisty back here with lots of roots and you can't see the trail that well unless you know it. I swerve around some mounds that kids use to dirt-jump and park behind this big fallen tree. Misty stops by the mounds and I see her eyeing them like *Hmmm, I should maybe jump this.*

"You will definitely get hurt," I say.

"I bet I could do it."

I sit on the fallen tree. "Yeah, but you're not allowed to play contact sports. If you fall you're going to make contact with the ground."

Misty leans her bike against the tree and sits next to

me. There's some Velcro ripping as she takes off her wrist guards. I don't even know how she grips the handlebars with those things on.

"Tell me a joke."

"What?"

"You used to say funny stuff," she says. "They were burns but not like mean. You just liked to make jokes."

"You say it like we used to hang out all the time."

"Not all the time," she says. "But sometimes. I mean, if I was outside and you were outside I'd wave and you'd wave back. Or if I threw something in the Mitchells' yard sometimes you'd see it and go get it for me."

I try to find that in my brain.

"That was like one time," I say.

"No. It was more than that."

A plane flies overhead. I think about all the people who will be flying near Yellowstone in two weeks and hope they lose their tickets or get stuck in traffic and miss the flight. "Do you think I'm a big jerk?"

She looks at me. "How big?"

"So you do."

"No."

"Hmm."

Misty takes her helmet off and loosens the strap. "A big jerk is somebody who's mostly mean all over. More than fifty percent of them is mean. That's a big jerk. A Real Jerk."

"So what am I?"

"Maybe twenty percent."

I grab this big stick and poke at the dead tree's roots. They look so weird out of the ground like this. "How come it's always me who's the jerk? Maybe other people are jerks and I'm the normal one."

"Like who?"

"My dad is a jerk. He's way over fifty percent."

"He seems pretty nice."

"Yeah, that's because he's got a secret life you don't know about." I'm smacking the tree roots and getting lots of dirt to fall off. It feels amazing. "He thinks I don't know, but I know and so, yeah, he is a gigantic jerk."

Misty comes over and looks around for a stick. She finds one and starts hacking at the roots too. Her aim is off, but when she lands one it's serious. "What did he do?"

I go at the tree roots like a construction worker doing demo. I'm actually wondering if I could maybe clear this whole stump of dirt. Misty picks up the pace too and we're just going wild, whacking and smacking and watching the dirt fall into the big hole where the roots used to be buried. When most of it is off, I toss my stick in the pit and get some water from my bike.

"He goes on these dates with women from the Internet," I say.

"All different women?"

"Maybe just a couple of the same ones. I don't know."

"Huh," she says. "That must be weird for you. That stinks."

"Yeah." I slap at the air to try and set an example of what will happen to other bugs who come near me. It doesn't work. "And then last night he wrecks movie roulette because he's already seen the one we watched with her and is texting her funny scenes during the movie."

"What's movie roulette?"

"It's this thing my—" I shake my head. "It's this stupid tradition we used to do. And I didn't even want to do it and then he wrecks it. Like, what's his problem?"

Misty's phone dings. She checks it and then starts putting her wrist guards back on. "You should tell him you hate him going out with Internet ladies."

"Like it would matter."

"You should still tell him." Misty buckles her helmet. "And I don't think he's a Real Jerk."

"What?"

"I mean, he's hiding it. He knows it might really make you mad. A Real Jerk would do it and not care what anybody thought."

"It's still messed up."

We get our bikes and walk them back through the woods. At the road she stops and says, "So."

"What?"

"That thing I wanted to ask you. To be continued."

"Oh. Right."

She grins and says, "I would like to be your official apocalypse assistant."

I blink. "What does that even mean?"

"I'll help you finish the shed and stuff. Give you suggestions to make it better. I think we'd make a good team."

I look at her for a couple seconds and then at the road. My throat hurts, like it's swollen. I swallow, but it still feels weird. "I don't think so."

"Why not? I can be pretty helpful."

"It's just a lot of specific stuff," I say. "I gotta do it."

She frowns. "You think I'll mess it up."

"It's just—I have to make sure it's exactly right. So I'm ready."

She watches me a couple more seconds. I look back at the road. She takes this breath and I think maybe she's going to ask again, and my throat hurts again, and I think maybe I should just nod and let her, because really the help would be kind of great.

"Okay." Misty gets on her bike. "Wanna keep riding?"

"Yeah."

We ride around the neighborhood for a while, talking about stupid stuff like Mr. Hines's giant beard and how much homework we have for just starting school. Misty doesn't tighten her helmet right, so it slides forward and blocks her eyes and she almost crashes into me. Maybe it's good she's not helping me finish the shed.

I just need to get that door on.

1

"**A**steroids," says Mrs. Baker, my science teacher. "Meteorites. All sorts of space junk. It's all careening toward us right now—and now." She snaps her fingers. "They cross in front of Earth's orbit daily, with little to no advance warning. Are you tracking with me?"

I nod. I know this stuff by heart.

"Even if we *could* know ahead of time—say, a few months—the geniuses at NASA aren't sure we could do anything about it. If an asteroid is coming at us, it's coming at us."

"Did one ever hit us?" Misty asks. Science is the only class we have together, but she's way up at the front.

"Hands, please," Mrs. Baker says.

Misty raises her hand real slow at first, then shoots it up. Some kids laugh and I smirk because *Come on, Mrs. Baker.* "Has something ever hit Earth before?"

"Yeah," I say. Mrs. Baker swings her head and I raise my hand normally. She nods and I say, "The Manson Crater, in Iowa. A big meteor hit and killed everything within a couple hundred miles."

"Correct. And a larger impact site known as KT was in

Mexico, near a region called the Yucatan. Scientists think that's the one that wiped out the dinosaurs." Mrs. Baker brings her hands together really big like an alligator chomping down. *"Kaboom!"* she yells. "Just like that. You tracking with me?"

Mrs. Baker starts going over the project guidelines, something about picking another planet to colonize. It's *blah blah blah* to me because I'm back millions of years ago at the Manson Crater impact, seeing the ash and debris turn five states into a fire pit. Then it explodes across America and scorches everything up in seconds just like the supervolcano will in eleven days and I feel my fingernails stabbing in my palms 'cause I'm making these crazy fists to stop the buzzing.

I get up to grab a laptop from the cart and it sort of goes away until I start googling stuff. Every article is about giant space junk pulverizing Earth and then I'm just back at the Manson Crater and the supervolcano. The End.

My student email dings an alert.

NEW MESSAGE FROM: MERCEDES KNOLL

I look up and see her turn back around like she wasn't just staring at me.

I click on the email.

Subject: Why I should be your assistant

Derrick,

Here's a list of skills that prove I'm the best candidate for the job of apocalypse assistant. Remember that I'm the only candidate, which makes me even better.

1. I have good attention to detail. Ask my sister Brynn about how I used to always beat her in those memory games where you have to pair two cards from a giant set.

2. I am a good conversationalist. That means I'm good at talking (I looked it up). This will help because you're not good at talking (you usually don't talk but get this blank look like you're mad or sad or both) and things might get boring while we work. Ask my parents about a road trip we took and they will back this up.

3. I never give up. Obviously this email is proof of that but also I survived a pretty serious kidney disease. I mean, that sounds like bragging but it's true. You can ask my doctors and nurses and this girl named Tanya who I shared a room with at CHOP. She got a new pair of lungs and moved to Arizona but we text so I could get you her number.

4. I am clever. Catching Pigeon is probably the best example. You were there so you don't need to ask Brynn, which would be a bad idea anyway because she's having nightmares where birds attack her.

5. Hatchet accuracy. Maybe there will be some wood chopping or something. This could come in handy I think.

Summary: From all the apocalypse movies and shows I've seen, these are good qualities to have. I hope you will consider my application and respond ASAP (as soon as possible) because you really don't have time to waste (lol lol).

Sincerely,
Misty

2

"**Y**ou saw me throw that hatchet," Misty says. We walk around a blob of seventh graders jamming up the hallway. "You know I'd be a good sidekick."

"I'm not fighting crime."

"Just saying that when things get ugly, you might want somebody who knows her way around a hatchet."

I duck out a side door to the courtyard. The library is on the other side and when it's hot out, our librarian, Mrs. Kimble, keeps the door open. She also lets me eat in there and read *Apocalypse Soon!* message boards instead of going to the cafeteria.

"I don't need any help," I say. And I mean it this time—not like yesterday. All that asteroid talk in science was a wake-up call. No way I'm leaving my safety up to anybody but me. "I'm almost done, anyway. My last thing is coming tomorrow."

"What is it?"

"A rolling steel door."

She jumps ahead and puts a hand out. "If I can think of one serious thing you forgot about—and offer a good solution—you have to let me help."

"Why do you even want to help?" I ask. "You don't believe It's happening."

"How do you know?"

"Because you didn't ask me to make room in the shed. If you thought it was the Real Deal, you'd want to get in."

She nods. Thinks about it. "Okay. You're right. But I don't have to believe you to help."

"I don't want any help." I walk past her. "I have to survive in it, so I'm gonna be the one to build it."

I'm at the library door when she shouts, *"Poop."*

It echoes around the courtyard. A couple rooms have their windows open and I hear kids laugh.

I turn around and say, "What?"

"Remember last year when we did the Civil War? Mr. Carrow said most soldiers died of disease and diarrhea. Do you really want to be killed by your own poop?"

"I have a system figured out."

"What is it?"

"None of your business."

"That joke stinks." Misty slaps her knee really hard like she knows that was the dumbest pun ever. "What is it?"

I check my watch. Five minutes of lunch already gone. "I'm going to take it out at night and bury it. Like when you go camping."

"But what about the smell, during the day? It's going to attract flies. Flies lead to disease."

I'm feeling a little sick to my stomach. "You go in a bag and sprinkle it with kitty litter. I bought one of those compost bins to put it in during the day. They hide the smell."

"What if you knock it over? It's kind of a small space."

"I won't knock it over," I say.

"If a bunch of people are trying to break into your shed, and it's the middle of the night, there's a good chance you kick that thing over. Poop everywhere."

"I'll be careful."

"As your doomsday assistant, I would recommend you consider the worst possible scenario and plan to avoid it."

"You're not my assistant."

"And if you keep ignoring my advice, I won't be."

"Good."

And then I turn and walk into the library.

Right into Mr. Killroy.

3

I slouch way down in his office and stare at the watermark on the ceiling. I think it's leaking into the next tile. Definitely getting bigger. I look outside the office and see Mr. Killroy standing with Misty. He's saying stuff and then he's writing her a pass.

"Am I in trouble?" I ask when he comes in. "Because I didn't scream *poop* in the courtyard. That was Misty."

"You're not in trouble." He sits down. "I was looking for you anyway."

"Why?"

"Just wanted to chat."

"About what?"

Mr. Killroy folds his hands. "About Thursday."

I'm looking at him, but doing that thing where I zone out and make his face all fuzzy. I'm thinking about the stupid heart Claudia drew on my calendar. "Did my dad ask you to do this?"

He doesn't say anything.

"Did he?"

"Yeah."

I slouch back down. Zone out at the ceiling and turn the watermark into a black puddle.

"So how are you feeling?" Mr. Killroy asks.

"Fine."

"Really?"

"Yeah."

I blink, and I'm in the desert movie. Ground shaking, dust storm building. Humvees barreling toward me and now there's a black hole opening up in the sky—that's something new. It morphs into the watermark, like this big giant black hole that's—

The phone on Mr. Killroy's desk rings and jolts me out of it. He hits a button and it stops. Looks at me real close and says, "Derrick."

"I'm fine." I wipe my forehead with my hand. Wet. "I'm fine. I just don't want to talk about it."

Mr. Killroy watches me for a couple seconds and then leans back. "Tell me about Misty. You two close?"

"Not really. Just live near each other."

"You were hanging out today."

"She was following me," I say. "Which is what she usually does. Just shows up, does weird stuff."

"Like what?"

I tell him about the hatchet throwing and the dangerous bike ramp making and the Pigeon catching and her Life Is a Buffet That Closes quest. He's smiling, which I didn't think he could do.

"She sounds like a lot of fun," he says. "And from talking to her, she seems like a good friend."

I look at him real quick. "What did she say?"

"Just that you're working on this big project. Something she wants to help with."

So she didn't tell him. Phew. "Yeah."

"So are you going to let her help?"

I shake my head. "I gotta do it myself."

Mr. Killroy nods. Thinks for a little or something, just sits there. Then he starts rolling up his sleeve—way up, all the way to his armpit almost. The big giant bicep of his right arm is out and he's holding it up to me like *Witness my big giant bicep.*

"See this?" he asks.

I lean back a little. "Uh."

He turns his arm some more and then I see it—a big scar running across this bicep. There's another one below the crook of his elbow. Both way darker than the other skin around it.

"Oh, man," I say. "Whoa."

He unrolls his shirtsleeve back down. "You know what spotting is?"

"No."

"It's when you lift weights with somebody else—you stick real close to them during the set. If they can't handle it, you step in to help. It's for safety."

"Okay."

"But when you're the strongest guy in the room, who

needs that?" He grunts. "I was bench-pressing one night in college, alone. Thought I was a real tough guy. But on the last repetition, I couldn't get the bar back up. I pushed so hard that my bicep tendon tore right off the elbow joint. Two hundred and twenty-five pounds was just sitting on my chest, slowly crushing me."

"How'd you get it off?"

"A janitor cleaning the locker room heard me screaming. He ran in and helped."

"Hmm."

Mr. Killroy buttons his cuff and smooths the sleeve out. "You get what I'm saying?"

I think about it and then say, "Don't lift weights."

He smirks. Throws an eyebrow up and starts writing me a pass back to class. "Don't lift weights by yourself."

4

On the way home I hang my arm out the window and make a wing with my hand. I'm picturing Mr. Killroy in the gym, his arm hanging all weird from the ripped bicep. I wonder if he cried. I can't picture that.

"Dee," Claudia says.

"Uh-huh."

"Dad and I are going to the cemetery on Thursday. We want you to come."

I tilt my hand forward and the air shoves it down—way faster than when I tilt it up. "Why?"

"What kind of question is that? Because She's our mom."

I look over at her. "Maybe Dad will bring one of his Internet girlfriends. We'll go around the circle sharing family memories, but when it lands on her, things will get really awkward."

"Do it for me."

I think of how mad she was about me ruining movie night—even though it wasn't really me. It was *him*. The Real Jerk.

"So you're coming?" she asks.

"Fine," I say. "But I'm not saying anything."

1

"**H**ad you been in downtown Manhattan on that day, you might have thought the world was ending."

Mr. Hines goes to the next image on his 9/11 Power-Point. A bunch of people are in the middle of a city street, totally covered in white dust. Some of them have cuts on their faces. They all look dazed and confused. One lady is crying.

"Two thousand nine hundred seventy-seven people died during the terrorist attacks that day," he says. "Hundreds more from lung cancer and respiratory diseases related to debris inhalation. It remains the deadliest attack on American soil in our country's history."

The class is silent. I look around and see them all sucked in by the photo slideshow.

"They didn't *die*."

I think, *Yeah, they didn't just die,* and look for whoever said it, but people are looking at me. Mr. Hines is looking at me too, and I'm sweating a little, wondering how what I was thinking came out of my mouth.

"What's that?" Mr. Hines asks.

"They were killed," I say. "They didn't just die. Somebody killed them."

Mr. Hines strokes his big black beard. "You're right."

"And other people were killed because of this too." *Jeez,* I can't shut up. And it's like a sauna in here. "Lots of people in Iraq and Afghanistan."

"Yes," Mr. Hines says.

"Some of them weren't even soldiers," I say. Am I yelling? Kids are turning in their chairs to get a better look at me. "They weren't fighting, but they still got killed."

"Yes, they did." Mr. Hines leans against the whiteboard and folds his arms. It's like he's waiting for more, but that's all I've got. I think. "Last year you studied the Civil War, remember? There was a general who said 'War is cruelty.'" He looks around to the kids nodding, but ends up back at me. "I think that's about the truest thing a person could say about it. Everybody loses."

I pick the plastic edges of my binder. Sort of feels like I'm sliding to one side. I really want to disappear. Mr. Hines passes out a background reading on 9/11. My phone buzzes in my pocket.

UPS Update: Your package is arriving today.

Instead of doing the worksheet, I find an online version of the steel door manual and start reading.

2

I'm waiting in the garage when the UPS guy pulls up.

"Got a big one today," he says.

"Yeah."

He drags out this giant rectangular box and scans it.

"Need help?" he asks, but I'm already dragging it around back.

I lay it down under the maple tree and rip open the box. I line up all the parts, make sure everything is here, and start reading the directions. It's almost four, which gives me about three and a half hours of daylight to get this thing on.

"Did you get a rocket launcher?"

Misty comes out of nowhere and starts touching random pieces on the ground.

"It's the door I told you about." I get up and take a couple of bolts from her hand. "Come on. Stop."

"What's wrong with the doors that are on there?"

"Hinge doors have too many weak points. They could be forced open."

"Right." She claps her hands. "So what do we do first: Take the old ones off or build the new one?"

"I said I don't need your help."

"It's supposed to rain, you know. You could do it faster if I helped."

"Not until ten," I say. "My doomsday blog uses this special weather app. I got plenty of time."

I get my screwdriver and hammer out and start popping pins out of the old hinge doors. The first one comes off easy, but the next one is so rusted I have to unscrew the whole plate. It goes fine until the last screw flies out and the door falls on my foot.

"Crap!" Is it broken? No, I don't think so. I wiggle my toes and put weight on it. It's sore, but I can walk. I start on the second door, which comes off way easier.

"Fecal-borne pathogen," Misty says. She's in the shade, reading on her phone. "That's when flies land on your poop, then land on your plate. You're basically eating—"

"I get it."

I grab the two big steel brackets from my new door assembly and bring them in the shed. I lean one against the wall and line the other along the inside door frame. Using a clamp, I lock it in place and then drill all the pilot holes for the bolts that will secure it to the shed. I do the same to the other side and check my watch: *4:32 p.m.*

"How much money do you have left from your deck fixing gigs?" Misty asks.

"Almost six hundred bucks. Why?"

She walks over and shows me her phone. "The Poop

Master 5000: A Dry Flush Composting Toilet. Runs on lithium batteries. Five hundred bucks at Home Depot."

"Lithium batteries explode. No way I'm putting that in here."

"Only the phone ones exploded," Misty says. "Just check it out."

I scroll through the specs. It does look legit. "Hmm."

"Pretty good, huh?"

"I guess."

And then a raindrop hits the screen. *Splat.*

I look up and see this big black cloud rolling at us. "Where did that come from?"

Misty jerks her head back a little, then wipes her cheek. "Uh-oh."

"Crap," I say. Another drop hits me in the eye. *"Crap."*

"What do we do?" Misty says real loud. The wind has picked up. I can see deck umbrellas starting to bend. "Put the old doors back on?"

"We can't. The hinge is bent." *Crap.* I picture the shed getting soaked and moldy and turning into a bacteria biohazard and I'm breathing so hard but can't get enough air.

Why wasn't I more careful? And how did my weather app get it wrong?

This is a disaster.

And then Misty sprints toward my house. Her ponytail whips back and forth against her head as she bolts around the side to the front. It's starting to rain now, for real, getting heavier by the second. Most of the steel door stuff is laid out under the maple tree, but that won't protect it for long. I start hauling it by the armful into the shed. I've got most of it in when Misty runs back with a giant blue tarp.

"Grab the corner!" she yells above the rain. It's straight-up pouring now, dripping off our faces.

I duck into the shed where my toolbox is to grab the staple gun. I take the loose corner and drape it above the left side, stapling like crazy. It's ugly, but it should keep most of the stuff dry until the storm passes.

"Some is still getting in," Misty shouts, pointing to the floor.

She's gone again, then back in seconds with another tarp. I fold it long ways and lay it down by the opening to keep the floor dry.

"How did you know where these were?" I ask.

"I saw them the other night. After I tried to rob you."

"Right."

She looks around the edges for water. "I think it's good. I think we got it."

I dig into a crate and take out a camping towel that absorbs water like a sponge. I go to wipe my face, but see Misty wringing water from her ponytail with two hands.

"Here."

She wipes her face and gives it back. "Thanks."

I dry off, and we sit on the floor, listening to the rain beat on the roof. She lifts the tarp to peek out and watch the storm, and I see her smiling like this is the best day of her life. I've seen her do that before, I think. Smiling wide, laughing. Hanging out by the shed.

Her hand gripping the wagon handle.

1

I'm in the desert.

The mountains are extra pretty today. But the sky is weird: It's ceiling tiles instead of that blue going on forever. The watermark from Mr. Killroy's office is spreading and turning black and then there's an explosion—but it's not the *KABOOM* I'm expecting on September 21.

It's a *Whoooooooooooook!*

Like an alarm.

No—a siren.

The *Apocalypse Soon!* air raid siren.

The one that gets pushed out to all members when an "Apocalyptic Event" goes down in the world.

Whoooooooooooook!

I jump out of bed and fall on my face in the dark room.

Whoooooooooooook!

This is happening.

It's happening.

I claw for shoes in the dark but can't feel my fingers— totally numb. How much time have I lost already? Ten seconds? Twenty? I grab my go bag from the bedpost and tear it open, throwing on my headlamp. Drop it twice. Lunge for the door and fall because the room is like rotating weird. I crawl for the door and finally get up and sprint downstairs.

Whoooooooooooooooooooook!

Whoooooooooooooooooooook!

Whoooooooooooooooooooook!

I'm halfway across the yard when I see it.

The tarp.

No.

My heart skips three times, real fast. Stuff tilts again and the air is super-thick and I'm taking these big giant gasps to get more. I dive through the tarp where the doors used to be and strap on a gas mask. I'm choking now and it fogs up so I can barely see enough to put on my hazmat suit. I'm shaking pretty good and I can hear myself crying, which is weird because I don't feel like I'm crying but I definitely feel like I'm on fire. Part of my brain is still in the desert with the watermarked ceiling and I'm thinking, *Mr. Killroy really needs to get that leak fixed.*

Somebody grabs my arm. I scream. I kick and punch but they keep grabbing me and all I'm thinking is, *The door the door the door. This is all because I didn't put on the door.* I'm hitting the person but they're too strong and now they've tackled me to the ground and I can't get away. Their arms are like cement and I'm totally outmatched and so I just give in because it's obviously already over and this is The End and I wasn't ready. My mask gets ripped off and now I can really hear myself scream, and yeah, I'm definitely crying.

But somebody else is too.

Claudia.

She's standing outside the shed, hand on her mouth, watching my dad hold me down. He drags me onto the cot, telling me that nothing's wrong. I reach for my phone and see EARTHQUAKE: MEXICO, 5.8 MAGNITUDE.

Air comes back into my lungs. The tilting sort of levels out.

My dad's panting. It mixes with Claudia's whimpers like some awful soundtrack to The End of the World and I shove my hands over my ears. I curl up on my side and see that black knot spiraling out on the wall, ruining a perfectly good plank. I should've knocked it out before I started.

I should've gotten that door on.

2

I wake up and stare at the clock on my night table. *9:03 a.m.* Blink a couple times and then it all comes back and I shut them. How can you be dizzy lying down? I take this giant breath and let it out slow and sit up. Feels like I've been drugged. There's banging downstairs in the kitchen and it smells like bacon. My phone has a bunch of messages from Brock and Tommy saying they hope I feel better.

I shower and change and log onto *Apocalypse Soon!* to see what the crap happened. The message boards are crammed and some of them are still freaking out but mostly everybody is angry. My in-box has a message from the website admins that is this big long apology about what happened. Apparently there were two other smaller quakes along a fault line in the Indian Ocean, which triggered some superfancy tsunami warning that the admins also follow, and they got jumpy and sent out the air raid. To make up for it, they gave everybody a couple free months of membership.

So it wasn't The End.

But I've got a bigger problem—I wasn't ready.

If last night had been The End, I would be like everybody else.

Unprepared.

Gone.

My stomach grumbles because that bacon is smelling pretty amazing. I go downstairs and my dad is at the stove cooking eggs.

"Hey," he says.

"Hey."

A giant plate of bacon is on the counter and I sit on the stool and start eating it. It's amazing but still hot and I have to take it easy because I'm scorching my throat. I cough a little and get some water and then keep eating.

"How'd you sleep?" he asks.

"Okay."

"Thought you could use a day off."

"Yeah."

He puts some eggs on a plate and slides it across the island to me. Maybe this is the best breakfast ever.

"You want to talk about what happened?"

I chew for a while. Shake my head.

He drinks his coffee and watches me. "I called Dr. Mike."

"What?"

"Derrick—come on."

I stare at my eggs and bacon and keep eating. "I'm okay now. It was just a mistake."

"What was a mistake?"

"This thing—it's not a big deal."

He takes this big giant breath in and lets it out slow through his nose. "He has an opening today."

"I'm fine."

"Really?"

"I don't need to talk to Dr. Mike. He can't help me."

My dad dumps his coffee out and stares at the kitchen window. Maybe he's looking at the shed. I am, through the back slider, and I can't wait to get out there and put on that stupid door.

"I want you to take the day off," he says.

"Yeah." Perfect, actually. I'll have that door installed by lunch. "I think that's a good idea."

"From everything," he says. "School and the shed. And that website you follow. I want you to just rest today."

I drop my fork and it goes *clang* real loud on the plate. "What? Why?"

"Derrick."

"Dad, you don't get it—last night was a mistake. The guys who run the website messed up and so I thought It was happening. But it wasn't, so I'm fine. I just need—it will take me like an hour to install that door. Probably less."

He shakes his head and my stomach is sort of cramping hard and all that bacon is feeling not so good. I can see the tarp over the shed door through the back slider and it's starting to spin to one side and I can hear somebody screaming *Fine* and it's me and then I'm stomping upstairs and grabbing my schoolbag. My dad follows me and stands in my doorway.

"What are you doing?"

"Going to school," I say.

"Derrick—"

"What, I can't go to school?" Yelling again. I shove past him and head for the garage and grab my bike. Take a day off this close to The End? What an idiot.

"I'll drive you," he says. "Okay? I'll drive you."

"I'm fine."

"I'm going to drive you!" he yells.

I freeze. This is new, and sort of weird. He's standing there with his hands on his hips just watching me.

"Okay," I say, and put my bike back. He goes to get the keys and I head out to the truck, using my phone to find the door manual on Google.

I slam the mouse down because these library computers are the slowest ever. I couldn't read the manual on my phone and it won't load here.

"Everything okay?" Mrs. Kimble asks. She's behind her big circular desk checking in a mountain of books.

"Computer froze," I say.

"Try . . ." But I'm tuning her out, opening a new browser because that's what all the teachers say when something doesn't work. Still not loading. I should've just brought the actual manual with me. I probably could have run back to the shed real quick and grabbed it before my dad said anything. And what would he do anyway? Yell again? That was pretty weird.

"Dude." Somebody waves a hand in front of my face. "Yo."

I look up and see Brock. "Hey."

"Claudia said you were out sick when she picked us up this morning."

"Yeah. I'm feeling better."

Tommy sits down next to me and says, "Your face is, like, all weird. Like you're tired."

"Uh-huh."

"I was wondering." He's so close I can smell his lunch breath. "I was thinking."

I try a third browser. The page starts loading but then totally freezes on a white screen. "Mmhm."

"If you, like, wanted to borrow Pete. For Thursday."

"What?"

A kid walking by points at Tommy and does this weird motion like he's hammering something. Tommy laughs and gives the kid a thumbs-up. Then he says, "At movie night Claudia said something about—you guys were going to the cemetery on Thursday."

I stare at the screen. There's a tiny dot in the center that's maybe a speck. I try to smudge it off but it won't come off. It's like a busted pixel inside the busted computer. I keep poking and wiping, but it's not coming off. The monitor is shaking and ready to fall off.

"Pete's good company," Tommy says. "He doesn't say or do much, but that's cool. You know, like, just to have there. So you're not by yourself."

The screen unfreezes. Starts loading the manual real slow. "My sister and dad are going," I say.

"Yeah, but—people do it with dogs, I read. It's calming and stuff."

"Nah."

"I got a carrying bag," Tommy says. "I can bring him over before you go."

I shake my head. "Thanks. I'm okay."

Another kid walks by and does that hammer-swinging

motion to Tommy. He doesn't laugh or give a thumbs-up this time.

"You missed a good scrimmage," Brock says to me. "Those Union Middle School punks were begging for mercy by the end."

"Oh yeah. Sorry."

"Yeah yeah yeah," Tommy says. "It's cool."

"They're calling Tommy the Hammer," Brock says. He does that hammer thing the two kids did. "Because he crushes the other team's offense. Like a hammer. We're planning a whole bunch of new signs for the next game."

"Nice." The page finally loads and I start reading.

"Lunch is over, boys," Mrs. Kimble says.

Crap.

I hit PRINT and go to the copier to pick it up. Tommy and Brock follow me.

"We're making them at my house on Friday," Brock says. "Brock dogs will be served."

"Okay."

"I love Brock dogs," Tommy says.

"Everybody loves Brock dogs." We go to leave and Brock holds the door open so a couple seventh graders can come in. He blocks it when I try to go through. "So you're coming, right? Friday?"

"Yeah." I count the pages to make sure they're all there. "Yeah. Friday."

"Dude." He says it weird and looks away for a second. "Are you okay?"

"What? Yeah."

He frowns or something and then goes out the door to class.

4

I take the bus home because it's faster than waiting for Claudia. I sit in the front so I can be the first one off at my stop.

The door is going on *today*.

I will be ready.

Today.

I get off the bus and sprint down the sidewalk to my house. I don't even change—just drop my stuff in the garage and grab my tools and head back to the—

"No."

The blue tarp is gone.

My bins and stuff are all over the lawn.

Things go wobbly. My brain can't figure out what is happening but then it figures out exactly what is happening: People got to my stuff. Somebody must've seen it and raided my supplies during the day and now it's all gone.

I'm making this weird sound, but it's all echoey and now I'm like drifting toward the shed, all woozy. Why didn't I just stay home like my dad wanted me to? I could have guarded the shed and this wouldn't have happened—I could have called the police or something. Now it's all ruined. All my prep.

Gone.

Destroyed.

"Hey."

I can't really see that good, but I think that's Misty walking out of the shed and waving at me.

"Earth to Derrick," she says.

"What—what are you doing?"

"Waiting for you."

I walk over and look inside. Most of the stuff is back to normal, except for the bins outside.

But no—something is different.

A giant something.

The new steel door.

It's on.

"Oh, man," I say. "What?"

"Pretty sweet, huh?"

The door is rolled up in a tight coil at the top of the opening. "You installed it? How?"

"I mean, you made the pilot holes, and you left the directions." She shrugs. "The company has a whole video walkthrough on their website, so I just watched that a bunch of times."

I scan all the bolts she put on, then grab my adjustable wrench and check their tension.

"They're not too tight," she says. "The guy on the video kept saying how bad overtightening is. By the third time I was like, *Buddy, we get it.*"

I still check them.

"Good?" she asks.

"Yeah." I get my level and check to make sure the brackets are straight, and then go outside to see if there are any parts left over. Maybe she skipped something.

But no. Just a couple extra bolts they give you in case you lose some.

"Does it work?" I ask.

"I was waiting for you to try it."

We go in the shed and each grab a side. The door unrolls easily at first, but gets tough toward the bottom. I fix the spring tension and it unrolls the whole way. The shed goes dark.

"Derrick."

"Yeah."

"This is kind of freaking me out."

"Sorry."

I feel for the overhead lamp and switch it on. I check every square inch of the door again.

"Misty," I say. "It's amazing."

"You're probably not super happy."

"Yeah. I mean, no." I shake my head. "Thanks. Really."

She does this bow from like the Middle Ages—lots of wide hand motions and bending way down at the waist. "Sure."

A couple seconds go by. "Why did you do this?" I ask.

She doesn't answer right away. "I was up this morning. Early."

"Okay."

"I heard lots of yelling, so I came out and—I thought—I thought somebody was trying to steal your stuff."

My stomach knots. "Mmhm."

"I've had one of those. Panic attacks. I know how scary they can be."

I'm looking past her at the shadows. My eyes feel really weird, like they're full or something and if I look right at her I'll blink and tons of liquid will come out.

"Yeah," I say.

"Sorry that it happened."

"Uh-huh."

"What actually happened?"

I say something, but it's all groggy and I clear my throat. "The guys who run my doomsday website sent out a false alarm about some earthquakes."

"That's good, I guess. That they were wrong."

"Yeah." I look back at her and say, "Thanks for—" but it's stuck in my throat.

And then Misty hugs me.

I just stand there because my arms are kind of pinned down, and if I move them she might think I'm trying to break up the hug, which I'm not, but not because I like Misty or something and we're going to start going out in my shed. It's not even close to that, but I don't know what it is. It's just a hug.

"I'm sorry about last night," she says.

"Yeah."

"And I'm sorry about your mom dying. I never got to tell you that."

"Uh-huh."

She gives a sort of ending-the-hug squeeze and steps back. We stare at each other for a while and then I say, "You can be my assistant," right as she says, "I just like you as a friend," and then we both laugh real awkwardly.

1

"**S**o I'll pick you up right after school." Claudia pushes her cereal around with a spoon. Her hair is kind of messy and her eyes are red like she didn't sleep. "Bus loop."

"Yeah."

She's staring at the bowl like it's a book. "Bus loop."

"You said that."

She takes it to the sink and dumps it in the garbage disposal. I don't think she ate any of it. "Listen: I know this is going to be hard for you."

"It's fine. I'm good." And it's not a lie. We got the door on. I don't want to go to the cemetery, but it won't take that long. "Are you okay?"

"Oh yeah. I'm fine. We're all just fine."

I rinse my bowl and stand there with her for a little, looking out the window. "You're a good sister slash mom."

She rubs her eyes. "Thanks."

I get my backpack and wait in the car. Misty comes out with her sister but walks over to our Subaru and gets in.

"Is it cool if I ride with you? I thought we could talk about exploding batteries."

"Sure."

She hands me an article printed from the Internet. Highlighting everywhere. "So I looked up all those exploding cell phones from last year. The ones with lithium batteries in them."

"Right."

"I spent most of the night reading every Poop Master 5000 review. No exploding issues. One guy in Michigan said his clogged, but I bet he put something down it he shouldn't have."

"That's good."

She takes the papers back. "I am giving the Poop Master 5000 my stamp of approval."

"Nice. Witness you slaying this meeting."

Misty points at me real quick. "That—right there."

"What?"

"The old you. The funny Derrick."

"Hmm."

She pulls out her phone. "The Home Depot by school has five in stock. I say we go today."

"Okay, good—wait. Crap. I can't."

"Oh, does Tommy have a game?"

"Uh." I can see the one wing of that stupid Air Force sticker on the glove compartment. "We're going to the cemetery. It's . . . today's a year."

Misty waits a second. "Of her—of when she—"

I nod.

"Are you okay?"

"Mmhm."

She watches me. "So, should we get it Friday?"

"Yeah." *Ugh.* Crap. "Wait—I'm making signs for Tommy's game at Brock's house."

"So Saturday."

"Yeah. Saturday."

Misty clicks the screen and puts the phone to her ear. "I'll reserve it, just in case anybody else around here is doing last-minute apocalypse prep."

"Good thinking."

"Hiring me was the best thing you ever did."

"I'd give you a raise, if I was actually paying you."

Misty points at me again. She mouths *Funny Derrick* as somebody on the other end picks up.

2

"Just ask him," Brock tells Tommy at lunch.

"Ask me what?"

Tommy chews on a gluten-free bagel. "It's about The End of the World."

"What about It?"

Tommy leans across the lunch table and says, "And it's about Pete."

"He wants you to make room for Pete in the shed," Brock says.

I look at them both. "Hmm."

"I'm just, like, worried," Tommy says.

"About what?"

"Well—you'll be, like . . ." Tommy looks at Brock, who does that frowning thing at his food. "You're gonna be lonely."

"I'll be okay."

Tommy digs out his phone and scrolls. "I read this thing, like, about how being alone can be bad for you. You can die from it."

"That's not true," I say. "I'll be fine."

He slides his phone to me and I pretend to read it for a minute. He says, "See?"

"It's fine." I give it back to him. "Plus he's your best friend. You'd miss him."

Tommy chews on a fingernail.

"And I don't know if there's room," I say. "His cage is pretty big."

"Yeah yeah yeah."

"It's not that big," Brock says. "You could make room."

"What about food?" I ask.

"Yeah, what about food," Tommy says. "You're right. It's stupid."

"We could get you a bunch of mice, ahead of time," Brock says. He elbows Tommy. "Couldn't we? A couple months' worth?"

Tommy nods. "Yeah. Maybe."

"Where would the mice go?" I ask.

"You could make room for them too," Brock says.

"What do I feed them?"

"They don't eat much," Tommy says. "Like, a tiny bit. I have that food too."

"So I'm taking care of a giant snake and a bunch of mice."

"Pete and his dinner are keeping you company," Brock says. It's sort of loud. "And it won't be for that long, maybe. If the volcano doesn't erupt, then Tommy will just take Pete back."

I stare at my tray. I'm just getting the shed finished and now they want to turn it into a reptile zoo.

"What if he gets out?" I ask Brock, because he's the one

pushing this super hard. "He'll eat me. You're always saying that to Tommy."

"Build a box to put the cage in," Brock says. "It'll be fine."

"Guys." Tommy shakes his head. "Whatever. It's cool."

Mr. Killroy gives the cleanup call and we dump our trash. Brock is right behind me and says, "You built a doomsday shelter. Can't you build a box to hold a snake cage?"

"It's really packed in there already," I say. "You've seen it."

"Dude."

Tommy is a couple feet ahead and hears us but looks away. A kid bumps into me, and then I bump into Brock. He kind of pushes me back with his shoulder and I sort of shove him back and then we're just staring at each other, and he's doing that frowning scowl thing. He shakes his head and says, "Just build the box, Dee."

"I—"

"Build it." He shakes his head at me and drops his tray on the big stack.

3

I wait for Claudia at the bus loop. What the heck is Brock's problem? A giant predator in my shed? Cramming even more stuff in there?

Stupid.

Claudia pulls up and I see the flowers on the front seat. The light hits them straight and they're so pretty, but there's this reflection right next to that sticker on the glove box.

"Dee," Claudia says.

"I'm coming."

I climb in the back and put my earbuds in to listen to this *Apocalypse Soon!* podcast on survival tips. I already know them, but it keeps me from looking at those stupid Air Force wings. Claudia doesn't say anything the whole drive, just grips the steering wheel like she's trying to yank it off. She makes really sharp turns that send me jerking all over the place.

It takes like a half hour to get to Washington Crossing National Cemetery. Claudia winds around a really long lane and parks on the side of the road behind my dad's truck. No other cars around. No people but us. I see him standing across the road in the half-circled wall thing that stores these tiny boxes of ashes from people in the military. His back is to us and his head is down. I wonder if he's going to yell at me again.

"You got this," Claudia says. Who is she talking to? Herself? "You're going to be fine."

She grabs the flowers and we walk across the road.

"Hey, Dad," she says. Gives him a hug.

"Hi, baby." He puts the flowers down near The Box that says WATERS, L. MAJOR. USAF. He's dressed sort of nice. "They're beautiful."

I stare at the ground because The Box makes my stomach ache. The humidity is pretty bad and my shirt is sticking to my back. I want out of here. I want to be back in the shed with the rolling steel door shut and locked, and no stupid giant snake in there with me.

After a while Claudia says, "Miss you, Mom. I'm applying to Penn State. Maybe they'll put me in the same dorm as you." Her voice wobbles on *same*. "I'm still thinking elementary education."

She touches The Box and does some crying. A fly lands on my face and I just let it do whatever. Anything to not think about The Box.

"They finally tore down that diner on York Road," my dad tells The Box. "Got bought up in less than a day— Sam's company. He bid the job out, but I knew he'd give it to me. You always used to say I should just get the guys together one night and do it myself." He laughs a little.

"It's going to be a garden center, if you can believe it."

The fly crawls across the bridge of my nose. It's lucky it's not on Brock's face.

Claudia nudges me.

I shake my head.

"Come on," she says.

"No."

She sighs real heavy and puts an arm around me. She hooks the other one in my dad's. The fly crawls in my ear and is probably trying to lay eggs, so I shake my head and it flies away. Something like five minutes goes by and then Claudia and my dad are hugging, and then he tries to hug me. I step back to avoid it and get this weird whiff coming off his shirt. It's girly and I've never smelled it before, so it can't be Claudia's—not that I go around smelling my sister.

This is new.

It's heavy and sweet, like flowers that are showing off. Like perfume.

I shove him back.

"Whoa," he says.

I'm balling up my fists. I move toward him and he's stepping back, pressed against other boxes, and Claudia is shouting, *"Derrick! Stop! Derrick—!"*

I don't even know what to say, and I don't have to—my dad knows. He could easily shove me back but he doesn't. He just stares, eyes wide with this face like *I'm so busted.*

I slam my palm against a box next to his head. The impact sends a sting up to my neck that's probably way worse than it feels 'cause of all the rage. I start walking back to the car.

"Derrick!" Claudia says.

"He was with one of them!" I shout. "He was on a date before he came here."

"What—what are you talking about?"

I march back a couple steps and point at him—that Real Jerk who has the guts to be within a mile of his girlfriends before visiting The Box. *"Ask him!"*

Claudia looks at my dad.

He looks at the ground. Rubs a hand over his jaw.

Guilty.

"This is so messed up you don't even know," I yell at him. *"You don't even know!"*

"Stop it," Claudia says. She's crying again. "Just stop—Dee."

"You should have just brought her," I shout. "Maybe let her say how sorry she is—"

"Shut up!" Claudia shrieks.

I walk to the car and get in the back seat. Slam the door and then kick it real hard three times *boom, boom, boom.* I see the wing tips on the glove compartment sticking out behind the headrest in front of me and punch the headrest.

Then I climb up and start peeling it off, digging and clawing and pulling until Claudia sees what I'm doing and sprints toward me yelling stuff that would get you suspended from school.

1

I get up really early so I don't have to see anyone. I eat Pop-Tarts, go out to the shed, and try to picture adding a big stupid box to hold a snake. Maybe it could fit. But only if I move all my bins around, which means totally rearranging how I get to all the stuff in an emergency.

Misty walks up the ramp carrying this big book. It has a picture of the sun on it.

"I'm going with Jupiter," she says. "It's huge. There has to be a place on it that humans can survive."

"What?"

"The colonization project for Mrs. Baker. Where humans should go if we can't live on Earth anymore. What planet are you doing?"

"I'm not."

"What?"

"It's due after the apocalypse."

"Huh." She shuts the book. "What are you measuring?"

"This thing for Tommy." I tell her about the snake box and the mice and the mice food.

"Cool," she says. "This place is turning into Noah's Ark."

"No. Not cool. It's gonna smell like snakes and mice."

"So you're not gonna do it?"

"No. I don't know." I shrug. "Brock is being a Real Jerk about it."

My phone buzzes. *I'm not driving you to school,* Claudia texts me. *Tell your friends.*

Ugh.

I text Brock and Tommy to take the bus. "I can't give you a ride," I tell Misty. "Claudia and I are in this big fight."

"About what?"

"I yelled at my dad at the cemetery yesterday."

"Why?"

"Because he's the Ultimate Real Jerk."

"Right, but why?"

I sit on the cot and pull the tape measure in and out. "He was with one of his girlfriends right before he came. And he didn't even deny it. How messed up is that?"

She thinks about it. "Pretty messed up."

"I told you he was a Real Jerk."

Misty nods. Then she opens her book and starts flipping pages. "There's this thing on Jupiter. It's called the Great Red Spot." She points to a picture of this giant red swirl on the planet's surface. "It's a storm, twice the size of Earth. Isn't that crazy? And it's been raging for hundreds of years. Nobody really knows how long it will last."

"Mmhm."

"You're like Jupiter."

"What?"

"You're kind of big for our grade. You can do lots of pushups."

"Okay."

Misty leans forward. She moves her hand in this big circle around my chest. "There's a storm in there. It's been raging a while and it's pretty strong."

My jaw feels weird, like I'm using a bunch of muscles up. I say, "Gotta get the bus," and walk out.

2

In science, Mrs. Baker gives us the whole period to work on our colony project. Instead, I find this website about NASA trying to save the world from the Yellowstone volcano. Their plan is to drill from the side way down and relieve the pressure, which sounds pretty cool and maybe could have worked except they aren't starting for a couple years.

My school email alert dings and I click on an email from Misty.

Subject: Ball pythons can bite

I think you should read this article. Tommy has a ball python right? They're not poisonous but a bunch of people on Google say they got bit by theirs and it hurt. They say you're not supposed to pull away because the teeth will sink in deeper or something so you just have to let it finish biting and then pry it off. It's in the article, check it out. Also here's a couple YouTube videos of people getting bit.

Sincerely,
Your apocalypse assistant

I read it and watch the videos. One guy is trying to show people how to pick up a snake without getting bit and gets bit a bunch of times.

I email back: I'm not gonna be picking him up if I do it but thanks.

A couple minutes later Misty emails me saying, This guy says you have to clean the vivarium (that's the official name for a snake house) every month. He says you have to take the snake out to do it right. Here's the link.

I read that one too. The guy has step-by-step pictures and the first one is *REMOVE YOUR SNAKE FROM THE VIVARIUM*. I picture Pete biting my hand or face and my fingers and then how snakes probably carry weird diseases so there could be infection and then I'm in big trouble.

I shut my laptop and walk it up to the cart. Misty points at her screen like *Come see this* but I go back to my seat because I'm already planning how to tell Brock, the Real Jerk, that I'm not building a stupid box for a snake that will probably try to eat me when I clean out his stupid vivarium.

3

"I 'm not building a stupid box for a snake that will probably try and eat me when I clean out his stupid vivarium," I tell Brock.

He uses a straw to make a bunch of holes in his hot dog and then squirts Cheez Whiz into them. "What's a vivarium?"

I'm outlining a poster on his basement carpet that says YOUR PARENTS WISH YOU WERE TOMMY. Tommy is in the bathroom upstairs having an allergy attack. "It's the glass thing where Pete lives."

"Just wear gloves," Brock says.

Ugh. "It's not that simple."

Brock takes a bite of his Brock dog and chews for a while. "I got two pairs for Christmas last year. You can have the extra. They're brand-new and real thick."

I shake my head. "I don't have time anyway."

"I thought the shed was done."

"I have to get this other thing tomorrow at Home Depot."

"What other thing?"

"This special toilet that you don't need water to use. It bags up your poop and turns it into compost."

Brock drips some Cheez Whiz on the poster and grabs

a paper towel, scrubbing it really hard. "So you can make room for a new toilet but not for Pete's box."

My chest is all swirly, and I think about Misty saying there's a storm in there. The Great Red Spot. "You don't get it."

"I don't get it?"

Tommy comes down the steps and starts playing FIFA on Brock's big-screen TV. I keep outlining, pushing the marker so hard it's like I'm carving the letters. It's real quiet for a while and then Brock says, "We're building the snake box tomorrow at Dee's house. Early, because he's busy later."

I stare up at him. The Great Red Spot gets going again, but then Tommy says, "Oh, cool," and looks at me over the couch like *This is so great*. I fake smile and keep tracing letters and wonder what the crap is wrong with Brock, The Ultra-Mega-Real Jerk.

"Let's do it at eight," Brock says. "So you can do your other thing."

"Yeah," I say.

I wait until Tommy is playing his game again to look at Brock like *Dude, what the crap is wrong with you.*

He just eats another Brock dog.

4

I push the earth in my room until the Great Red Spot goes away.

Stupid Brock.

Stupid snake box.

I'm starving because I was too mad to eat at Brock's. I hope Claudia doesn't feel like cooking so we can order pizza. I log into my savings account on my computer and check the balance to make sure I have enough money to cover the toilet tomorrow.

Good to go.

All I have to do is get the ATM card from my dad and have Misty's parents stop at the bank on the way. The stupid snake box shouldn't take more than an hour to make, so we could leave around nine. I text her, but she doesn't answer.

I cut across the Mitchells' backyard to her house and knock on their back slider. Her mom sees me and comes to the door.

"Hi, Derrick. How have you been?"

"Uh, good. Is Misty here?"

Her mom goes inside and shouts *Mercedes* up the steps, then comes back. "Been busy this summer with the deck work?"

"Uh-huh."

She smiles. Nods. "I bet you really miss us stealing your gasoline."

I nod. Then I say, "What?"

"I finally talked Scott into getting a bigger can so he's not always running out halfway through mowing the lawn anymore."

"Right," I say, but my face must be saying something else, because her face is like *Are you okay?*

Gasoline.

There's something on the lawn next to their deck. That red wagon. Black tires, white in the middle. Metal. Good for hauling heavy stuff around the yard.

Stealing your gasoline.

"Hey," Misty says, shoving her way through the door. "What's up?"

Her mom gives me another weird look and then shuts the slider.

"Uh." I shake my head to try and clear things out. "I was just checking what time your parents could take us to Home Depot tomorrow."

"I thought your dad was taking us."

"What? No."

"But he's got a truck."

"The toilet isn't that big. It can fit in any car."

She's shaking her head. "They're going to Brynn's swim meet. They barely let me stay home by myself."

"Oh, man."

"Why can't your dad take us?"

"No way."

"Why not?"

"Because I'm not asking him." I walk around and think it over. "I'd ask Claudia, but she wouldn't do it. She's still mad at me."

"What about Brock's or Tommy's parents?"

I give her a face like *Yeah right.*

"Then you gotta ask your dad."

I look over to my house and see Claudia carrying a pizza box onto our deck. My dad comes out with cups and a big bottle of soda.

"Ugh," I say. "Fine. We'll go right after the stupid snake box is done. Probably around nine."

"Okay."

I cut back across the Mitchells' yard and pull a chair up to our deck table. "Smells good."

"You eating with us?" Claudia asks.

"Yeah."

She looks at me for a second. "Okay. Go get a plate and a cup."

I come back and pour some soda. "Meat lovers. Nice."

My dad smiles like he should get an award.

Claudia puts the umbrella up so we're in the shade. It's humid but not that bad. They talk about work and school while I pick at my slice and dread having to ask my dad for help. Stupid Brynn. Is swimming even a sport?

"Dad," I say.

He cuts off whatever he was saying to Claudia. "Yeah?"

"I need—" Nope. "Can you give me and Misty a ride to Home Depot tomorrow?"

"Sure. Yeah. What time?"

"Nine, probably. Around nine."

"Yeah." He waits a couple seconds. "What are you buying?"

"There's this dry-flush toilet that runs on batteries. It's for the shed."

"That can't be cheap."

"I have the money."

"How much is it?" Claudia asks.

"Five hundred bucks."

She chokes on her soda. "Five *hundred* dollars?"

"Yeah, it's a really good one."

"You're gonna let him spend five *hundred* dollars on a toilet?" she says to my dad.

"I can do whatever I want with *my* money," I tell her.

"Dad. Are you serious?"

He rubs his face. Plays with a pizza crust. "He earned it."

Claudia gets up and gathers her plate and stuff. "It would be great if for just one second there was an actual parent in this house."

She goes inside and slams the slider shut.

My dad and I eat our pizza. I keep looking at him, but he's off somewhere in his head.

"So nine," I say.

He stays far away. "Yeah."

1

Tommy puts a pink pool noodle inside the rectangle outline I spray-painted on the grass.

"Why did you draw a face on it?" Misty asks him.

"Brock did that," Tommy says.

"I can't believe Kelly is letting you do this."

"I told her Derrick is thinking of getting a snake."

Brock walks over from the garage with a big piece of plywood. "We ready to start the frame?"

"Just measuring." I check my watch. Almost eight fifteen. "Okay, so is this good?"

"I think so." Tommy walks around the outline. "Should we measure again? Just to check?"

"It's fine."

Brock grabs an extra tape measure from my toolbox. He goes all around the outline, then compares it to some numbers on his phone. "I'd add two inches on each side so we can lift it in and out easier."

I shrug. "Fine."

Brock lets the tape measure curl up with a big *smack*. "It is fine. Now that we did it right."

Ugh.

I cut the frame boards and then screw them together. Brock measures the plywood sidings and cuts those, then we screw them on. Misty and Tommy stencil PETE'S CRIB on one side and LIVE SNAKE! DANGER! on the other. I check my watch every five seconds.

We finally set the plywood lid on top at *8:48*. Done. I start cleaning and Brock says, "What about hinges? And a lock?"

"What?"

He knocks on the lid. "So you can open it easier to feed him or clean it. And keep it secure."

"I vote for hinges and a lock too," Misty says. "I mean, this is the end of the world we're talking about. Things that could go wrong definitely will."

"Yeah," Tommy says. "Yeah yeah."

"I'll look for some in the garage," Brock says.

I hear my dad fire up the truck. "I'll find some and finish it later."

"Let's do it now."

"It's basically done."

"*No!*" Brock yells. It's pretty loud and I kind of jump. Even the birds shut up. "We're going to do it right—just like you've done everything else right so far for the shed."

Misty gives me the wide eyes. My mouth is moving, but it's not really me talking. It's the Great Red Jupiter Storm, and it's all tornado winds and debris.

"You need to freaking back off," I say. "These are my tools and my wood. I'll do what I want."

Brock walks up to me. "And I'm your friend. And I'm saying we're going to finish this like you said we would. The right way."

"Guys," Tommy says. "It's cool. We can do it later."

I make a face like *See?* and Brock clenches his jaw. He moves so quick I think he might be punching me, but no— he's picking up an extra board and hurling it like a spear at the—

Thud.

"Dude!" I scream. I two-hand shove him, but it's like pushing a boulder. I run to the shed and look at this big dent in the wall where the board hit. Not too deep, I don't think. But there's a tiny fracture that will get worse over time.

"What is your problem?" I yell, but Brock's stomping to the sidewalk. Tommy stands there for a couple seconds, looking at him and then at me. He's got a face like *Oh man oh man oh man* and then he's walking after him, that pink noodle dragging on the grass. He waves to me and then they walk away.

Misty comes over to the shed and checks out the damage. "Looks okay."

"Yeah, but like—what the crap?"

"He was acting like a Real Jerk."

"Right?"

"So were you."

"Me?"

"Mercedes!" We see her mom, standing in the yard, waving at us.

"What are you doing here?" Misty asks her. "Aren't you're supposed to be at the swim meet?"

"I need you to come here, please."

Misty walks over. Her mom says some stuff, and then Misty yells, and there's a lot of hand waving and finger pointing. Finally, Misty stomps inside, basically shutting the back slider in her mom's face.

2

"I thought Misty was coming with us," my dad says.

"Yeah. I think she got in trouble. I don't know."

The customer service line at Home Depot is ten people deep and there's like one lady working.

My dad says, "Are you two—you and Misty—"

"We're just friends."

"Right. . . . If you ever want to talk—"

"I'm good," I say, and seriously think of getting out of line.

He rubs his face. "That was Her . . . area."

I stare ahead and think about that Real Jerk, Brock. Maybe I should swap out that piece of plywood with a new one. But probably not enough time.

"What were you guys building out there this morning?" my dad asks.

"It's a box for Tommy's snake," I say. He gives me a weird look. "To beef up the cage he's in, so he can't get out."

"What kind of snake is it?"

"Ball python."

"Aren't they dangerous?"

Ugh. "Not really. But they can bite and wrap around stuff."

"Should probably put a lock on that cage."

Ugh.

Finally, we're at the counter.

"Hi," my dad says. The lady's name tag says *Brenda*. "We're picking up a reserved item."

"The Poop Master 5000," I say. "Under Derrick Waters."

Brenda types on the keyboard. "Hmm. Don't see it."

"What?"

"Could it be under another name?"

I clench my fists really hard a couple times. "Oh, wait— try Misty Knoll."

She types that in, then shakes her head. "Sorry."

"Okay, well, do you just have one we can get? There's five of them here."

"I see it's available through our online store."

"No." My voice sounds weird—far away. "She said it was here."

"Oh—now hold on." Brenda turns the screen toward me. "I see what happened. This is the Warrington, *Pennsylvania*, store—but there's another Warrington. In Idaho."

Stuff is tilting pretty fast. "Oh, man."

"So, no store around here has it?" my dad asks.

"I'm sorry, no," Brenda says.

He puts a hand on my shoulder, but I shake it off.

This can't be happening.

Isn't happening.

I try to breathe through my nose and fight the horrible poop scenarios playing out in my mind because it's fine.

It's fine.

It's fine.

I'll just use my old method.

But it was crappy, wasn't it? Fecal-borne pathogens trying to get me, flies buzzing around just loving it. And now I've got Pete and those mice doing their business in there too.

I need the Poop Master.

"Idaho," I say, and I'm gripping the counter pretty hard to stop the tilting. "Who even lives in Idaho? Is that even a real place—get *off* me!"

"Son, it's okay."

"It is *not* okay!" I shout. Everybody is staring at me. My eyes burn and the storm swirls in my chest and I'm pretty sure I'm gasping for air and going to pass out. I stumble out of line and make for the exit as the Great Red Spot spreads everywhere. Now I'm outside, my sweaty back against the hard brick of the biggest construction store in America that doesn't even have a freaking Poop Master 5000, except for that one store in Idaho.

This.

Is.

A.

Disaster.

No—this is *Misty's* disaster.

3

We get home and I see her walking out her front door with a backpack and headphones on. My dad pulls in the driveway and I'm out the door before he shuts the truck off.

"Idaho," I say, walking over. I'm definitely yelling, but she's not hearing me. *"Idaho!"*

Misty finally sees me and takes her headphones off. "What?"

"There's five Poop Master 5000s at the Home Depot in Warrington, *Idaho*. You had the wrong store."

"Really?"

"I don't have a toilet now. This is awful. And it's your fault."

"Sorry."

"Sorry?"

"Yeah—I'm sorry." Now she's yelling, and she's good at it. Better than me. "I made a mistake."

"You said you were good at details—it was the first point on your application thing."

"I didn't say I was perfect."

Her dad comes out. He's wearing one of those surgeon masks. He's got another one in his hand and he helps Misty put it on. Then he lifts a suitcase into the trunk.

My stomach is twisting up. "What's happening?"

Misty gets in the back seat and slams the door.

"Misty! What is happening?"

She puts her headphones back on and they drive away.

1

stare at the online order confirmation email for the Poop Master 5000. It's gonna be here in two days, because of my dad. I think he was so freaked out by my Home Depot scene that he paid extra for super-fast shipping.

At least I didn't have to ask him.

I click back to the manual. Says there's not much setup—I just have to plop it in the shed. I'm almost ready, actually for real. This is good.

But I feel sick. My intestines did epic battle the whole night and they're getting started again and I'm sweating pretty bad. I keep seeing Misty wearing that mask, driving away, and then I'm seeing her in the hospital, all those wires probably attached to her like before, when she was maybe not going to make it.

When she was waiting for The End.

I go into the bathroom and check my temperature. No fever. I try to drink water, but nope, there's a DO NOT ENTER sign in my stomach.

Claudia walks past me. "Are you sick?"

"No. I don't know. Maybe."

She feels my forehead. Then my neck. "Derrick, you're drenched." She gets a little paper cup full of water and makes me drink it, and then do it again.

I sit down on the tub ledge because I'm feeling sort of light-headed. "I think Misty is in trouble. I think maybe her kidney disease is back."

"What? Why?"

"She left yesterday out of nowhere. Everybody had on these masks. I don't know."

"Maybe she left because you yelled at her in front of the whole neighborhood," Claudia says.

My throat gets real tight. I hug my knees and look at the wall so she can't see me.

"Hey—whoa." Claudia bends down. "Dee—I was just kidding."

I blink a couple times until it's not blurry and say, "She said it was literally impossible to come back, but it did."

"You don't know that. I'll text her sister. You want me to?"

"Yeah, okay."

Claudia goes to her room and comes back a minute later. "Okay, I texted her."

"What did she say?"

"It's early. She's probably sleeping or at another swim meet. Don't worry."

"Yeah." I take a couple deep breaths. Claudia sits on the tub ledge with me. I say, "I'm not a Real Jerk, you know."

"I know, buddy." She rubs my back. "You're just wound too tight."

"Mmhm."

I hear somebody on the steps, and then my dad's standing in the door. He doesn't say anything, but I can see Claudia making some hand motions and mouthing something like *It's okay.*

"Dee," she says. "Dee. Dad and I want to talk."

"What?"

"Not about this. And not really in the bathroom."

I move a couple inches away from her. "Talk about what?"

"About you. Us. Stuff that's been going on."

I look at my dad. "I said I was sorry for freaking out at Home Depot."

"It's not just that," he says. "It's about you not being able to take a break from—"

Claudia puts a hand up to stop him.

"We want to see Dr. Mike," she says.

I stand up. "No. I'm not going back there. Dad already tried that."

"As a family, Dee. Not to talk about your stuff."

"What?"

"People do this," she says. "Family therapy. It's a thing. Dad and I think it could be really helpful for us."

I look at him, and then at Claudia. She's basically begging me with her eyes. "Fine. But I'm not gonna be saying a lot of stuff. Don't get mad if I just sit there."

Claudia hugs me. "Dad will call Dr. Mike and see when he can fit us in."

I'm thinking about Misty, staring at The End again.

2

I force-feed myself a Pop-Tart and look for hinges in the garage. Claudia swears she'll come get me as soon as Brynn texts her, so I'm staying busy until that happens. I can't find any hinges or a lock. Whatever. I'm not asking for a ride to Home Depot again. I'll just put something heavy on the lid to keep Pete from busting out.

I go back to the shed and rearrange everything. I keep checking my phone, but still no text. I peek out of the shed a lot because maybe Misty will just show up like always— just appear outside and say something random. It used to be annoying, but now it would be amazing.

I roll the steel door shut and sit in the dark for a while. It's pitch-black, so I don't even have to close my eyes to play the desert movie—it just pops on. The mountain peaks seem farther away, like they're not even real, but I know they are because this is an actual place. I only looked it up once on Google Earth, but this is what I saw and it's stuck in my brain.

The dust clouds at the far end of the road kick up and then the ground is rumbling and I'm thinking, *It's so pretty here, like nothing bad could ever happen.*

My phone buzzes and I rip it out of my pocket. I wipe sweat out of my eyes and read the text.

Misty is fine, Claudia says.

I stare at the phone. A car door slams outside, close. Ten seconds go by and I hear our back slider open.

"Did you see my text?" Claudia shouts at me from the deck.

I hear another door slam. Heavy, like maybe a trunk. I roll up the steel door and run to the edge of our yard so I can see Misty's driveway and there she is. Walking into her house. Headphones on.

Mask off.

"Dee," Claudia says, but I'm halfway through the Mitchells' yard. I'm walking to Misty's front door and now I'm sort of jogging. It's amazing—I feel amazing. I'm flying. I ring the doorbell and her mom answers.

"Oh—hey, Derrick." No mask on her either.

"Uh, hi. Is Misty here?"

"She just got back." Her mom goes to the steps and says, *"Mercedes?"*

No answer.

Her mom calls again and then I hear "What?" but not like the normal Misty. This Misty sounds like she just got off a roller coaster and is trying to find the bathroom.

"Derrick is here."

Nothing.

"Why don't you go up," her mom says.

I walk up the steps and stand outside her door. Last time

she said I couldn't come in, so I knock and say, "Hey, it's me."

Long pause. "Come in."

I open the door. Misty is laying index cards on the ground. Most of the carpet is covered. She lays a couple right in a row, then walks to the other corner and puts another one down, then another. I read some.

Jet Ski on the Delaware River.

Watch all the Princess Diaries *movies w/Brynn in 1 night.*

Make something huge disappear.

"You're not sick," I say. "I thought you were sick. Like maybe your kidney thing had come back."

"I told you it can't come back. Literally impossible. That's what I said."

"Yeah." I read a couple more cards on the ground.

Do the Ben & Jerry's ice cream challenge (the Vermonster).

Do a back flip.

Do a front flip.

Learn to whistle really loud with my fingers.

"Brynn ate peaches at a swim meet party," Misty says. "She's allergic." She keeps moving this one card to a different place—picking it up and putting it down. It says *Skydive.* "My parents thought it might be a cold or the flu, so I went to my gramma's in the city. Have to be careful."

"Oh." Then I say, "I didn't know peaches was an allergy."

Misty just keeps reading the cards and moving their spots.

"Sorry I freaked out about the toilet," I say. "Idaho. Pretty funny, when you think about it."

"Yeah."

"It's good that you're not sick. Again."

She ripples the index cards in her hands so it makes a *brrrrrrrrrr* sound. "I can't be your assistant anymore."

My stomach cramps a little. "Right. Yeah. Because I acted like a Real Jerk."

Misty looks at me real serious. The Stare. "I just can't anymore, okay?"

"Yeah. Okay. Well." I sort of wave. "See ya."

I'm basically out of her door when I see it—a shoebox on the ground with more index cards. Maybe thirty. The lid is right next to it. It says DONE. I look at it for a while, like maybe for a minute.

"People make mistakes," I say. "That's what you said. So you can keep being my assistant, even though I was a Real Jerk."

She doesn't say anything. I keep looking at the shoebox by my foot. There's an index card sticking out, and I can't read the whole thing, but I see the word *hatchet*. I'm squinting at it real hard and now I'm kneeling down to push the other cards away.

Hit a bull's-eye with a hatchet.

I grab another one that says *Play the bass cello* and then another that reads *Pry up a manhole cover.* Now I'm leafing through with both hands and Misty is saying "I just can't, okay," but I'm on this mission because it's here.

Life is a buffet, she said. *And it's gonna close at some point. So eat up.*

And there it is, in the middle. I pull it out and stand up. My hand is shaking.

Build a doomsday shelter.

"Derrick."

"Yeah."

"You don't get it."

Her handwriting is so neat. It could be a computer that did this, it's so neat. "Uh-huh."

"Just look around." She's stomping up and down the rows of cards, waving her arms. "I mean—*look!*"

"I get it."

"No—you don't get it." She's got that edge in her voice, like the next sentence is gonna be a scream. "Look at how many there are. And I've got another hundred in my head." She grabs a notebook off her desk and shows me the pages. They're all full. "Look at all these."

"Yeah."

"There's too many!" There's the scream. Man. She could out-freak me out. "Derrick. There's too many."

"We're almost done," I say. My eyes burn. "You could just

help me a couple more days and then—" but she's shaking her head, grabbing more notebooks and showing them to me.

"Every second has to count. You should get that."

I swallow, but it's hard, like a bunch of food is stuck. "What?"

"The apocalypse." She waves her hand toward the shed. "I mean, what if Brynn had the flu? And I got it, when I'm just getting started with my actual life? That could happen. I'd be back in that stupid hospital and all this—I couldn't do it."

I blink really hard so I can read the card again. "So I'm the new bass cello. There's something else cooler or not as boring."

"You don't know what it's like," Misty says.

"*I do!*" I yell, and then I'm down the steps, legs and arms pumping, lungs burning, out the door and sprinting to the shed, everything rumbling like when the Humvees in that desert movie come for me.

1

I fold my hazmat suit and put it in my school backpack. Zip it up and head downstairs. Claudia and my dad are talking real low and stop when I come in.

"Hey," she says.

I rip open a Pop-Tart bag and cram one in my mouth. "Am I taking the bus today?"

She shakes her head. My dad rubs his face.

"Dad is calling to see if Dr. Mike has any cancellations today," she says.

I shrug.

"Okay?"

"Yeah," I say, and head out to the Subaru. I unzip my book bag and check on the hazmat suit. Still there. I zip it back up and finish my Pop-Tart and hear Misty's door open. Brynn walks out and sees me and waves like *Oh hey I have a question* and starts walking over. Claudia comes out right then and now I'm getting out of the car and heading down the sidewalk toward the end of the street where some other kids are waiting.

"I'm taking the bus," I say.

"Derrick—" Claudia says.

But I'm gone and she doesn't follow me. I look back once and see her and Brynn looking at each other and saying stuff and shrugging and then Claudia gets in the car and drives toward Tommy's house.

2

I get off the bus and head for the closest bathroom. Ten seconds later I've got the hazmat suit on and heading for my locker, legit stopping traffic. Brock and Tommy are there and stare with their mouths open. Lots of kids whisper and smirk, but I don't care because this is the best I've felt at school in a long time.

Ready.

We say the pledge in homeroom but mostly everybody is looking at me instead of the flag. Mrs. Simons, my first-period algebra teacher, takes attendance and then the phone rings. She walks over and says real quiet, "Mr. Killroy wants to see you."

I walk down and head straight into his office.

"I don't want to talk," I say.

"Good." He shuts the door and says, "Because it's my turn. What are you wearing?"

"It's a hazmat suit."

"For the apocalypse," he says.

"How'd you know?"

"Your dad and I talk pretty regularly, Derrick—including this morning when I called him about your outfit. I know about your doomsday prepping." He waits. "I know about the shed."

My stomach knots and I'm seeing him bum-rush the shed—blowing right through the side and ripping all my bins out. Eating my stuff right there in the yard like a grizzly bear.

"So are you going to suspend me or what?" I ask.

"No."

"So can I go back to class?"

"No."

"Why not?"

"That suit is a distraction to every student and teacher." He leans forward, and I think he's going rip it off. "But not me. You'll stay next door in the guidance conference room until you decide to change. I'll email your teachers to send work down."

"Why don't you just send me home?"

"Your dad asked me not to."

Ugh. Big shocker.

"But that's not really why I called you down." He leans back. "I got a call from Misty Knoll's mom this morning."

I play with the elastic cuffs of the suit. "Uh-huh."

"She's refusing to come to school today, and her parents thought maybe you would know why."

"She's probably watching the *Princess Diaries*. Or Jet Skiing on the Delaware."

"What?"

"I don't know why she's not here." I shrug. "She's off,

okay. Way off. Like on another planet, in some other galaxy. She's basically an alien from another dimension."

"So you're still not friends."

"I told you: We just live near each other."

"Her mom said you've been spending a lot of time together." Mr. Killroy lowers his voice. "Maybe you're more than friends? But now you're not?"

"Ugh. No." Seriously. "Can't people just hang out and not like each other?"

"So you've been hanging out?"

I think about that stupid index card she wrote. How she put me in her DONE box like the stupid bass cello. "We used to hang out. We won't anymore."

"Why not?"

"Because she's a Real Jerk. She wasn't my friend two weeks ago, and she's not my friend now."

3

Mrs. Ruth comes into the guidance conference room at 2:10 and says, "Time to go, Derrick."

I grab my book bag and walk by Mr. Killroy's office. Empty. "To class?"

Then I see Claudia across the entryway, signing something in the main office. She waves at the secretaries and walks through the doors over to us. "Hey."

"What's going on?" I ask.

"Dr. Mike had a cancellation."

I shrug and walk out to the car. Better than sitting here another minute.

We drive twenty minutes through a ton of traffic and pull into a big shopping center. Dr. Mike's head-examiner office is in this medical building that looks like a giant bank. We walk through automatic sliding doors and pass a bunch of kid doctor offices, winding our way to a big waiting area with glass windows. My dad is already there, chatting with Dr. Mike. They both check out the hazmat suit but pretend not to.

"Hey, Derrick," Dr. Mike says. He looks the same: not really short or tall or fat or skinny. Still bald and probably still forty-something. "Good to see you again, buddy. You're huge."

"Yeah."

He opens another door and we follow him to his office. I sit in my normal chair across from a tiny couch and throw my feet up on the coffee table. He's added two more chairs on the ends of it where my dad and Claudia sit.

"Okay," Dr. Mike says. "Let's talk ground rules. Derrick: I'm not here to tell your dad or sister about our discussions, and they won't ask. Think of it like a completely separate thing. Think of us all as a new collective group, which might overlap with *some* of what you and I talked about before. Make sense?"

"Uh-huh," I say.

"Let's start simple: How did you feel about them asking to do this session?"

"It's fine."

"You agreed, so I assume you don't object."

I lean back and look at the ceiling. No watermark here. But there's something else. "What's that?"

He looks up. Everybody does. "What?"

My stomach feels weird. I point to a four-inch hole right above my head. Or is it six? "That."

"Oh—yeah. Maintenance guys replaced all the lights down here, something about efficiency ratings. They broke that one and had to take the whole housing out."

I stare at it for a while. "Hmm."

"So you don't object," Dr. Mike says.

"What?"

"To this session."

I swallow. Look away from the hole and play with my hazmat zipper. "It's fine."

"Okay." Dr. Mike looks at my dad and says, "Luke: You requested this session. Why don't you start."

After a long pause he says, "I need to apologize to my kids."

It's like a NOT BORED switch goes on inside me. I stare at him.

An apology.

Now we're talking.

"Apologize for what?" Dr. Mike asks.

"A couple things," he says. "I guess the first one is, I haven't been a very good parent since Laura passed."

"How so?"

He clears his throat. "I haven't been on top of things— parenting wise. Getting a sense of how they're doing with everything. I let them do their thing. I really backed off."

"You gave them significant independence," Dr. Mike says.

"But not in a good way."

"How so?"

He looks at the floor. "For one thing, I've let my daughter become the live-in maid. I didn't want it like that—Laura would kill me if she were here, because we shared those jobs. Laundry, dishes, cleaning—all of it. But I just let Claudia take them on."

"Dad." She reaches over and puts a hand on his arm.

I eye-roll because let's just get to the good stuff—the real reason he needs to apologize.

"I'm their father. I'm supposed to protect them when life turns bad. Support them—not disappear." He rubs his face so hard it sounds like somebody sanding a piece of wood. "This past year, I feel like I took their normal teenage life away—Claudia especially. And I feel awful."

Claudia wipes her eyes. He grabs her hand and they fumble for the right grip.

"Anything else?" Dr. Mike asks.

I sit up and lean forward a little. I wish we were filming this.

Here.

We.

Go.

"I let the shed go too far," he says. "I helped Derrick get this way."

It's silent, and then there's a ringing in my ear. I try to yell but can't get the words out—the Great Red Spot is sucking up all my air.

"I knew you were on those blogs," he says to me. "I let you use my credit card for the subscription. I just let it happen. I let it keep happening." He shakes his head. "And the shed—I shouldn't have let you change it. I'm your father, and I'm supposed to protect you, and I just enabled you. I didn't confront you or even try to help. I just let you build it. Everything that's happening with you is my fault."

"You're sorry about the shed?" My voice is shaking. Hands buzzing and heading for my face. I'm standing now, towering over him, and Dr. Mike is looking at me like *Oh no*. "The shed isn't the problem—*it's a solution*," I shout. "*You're* the problem—you going out with every lady on eHarmony. *That's the problem.*"

"*Derrick!*" Claudia yells.

"Stop defending him." I want to punch him so bad—a hundred times more than at the cemetery. Hit him in his stupid face like *boom boom boom*, but I'm not sure I could because this room is starting to slant pretty hard to one side. "And you're *not* touching the shed. It's mine. I built it with my own money, and you're not gonna touch it."

His hand is over his eyes now, like he's hiding his face. "Derrick."

"You—"

And now I'm cold, like ice. Super-dizzy and my heart is like skipping beats or something and going way too fast. In my head I see construction guys and bulldozers and hear the *beep-beep-beep* of their trucks backing onto our lawn.

"What did you do?" I ask.

He doesn't move.

"What did you do?" I say again, but it sounds like a really little kid, way littler than me, who is about to cry.

"Son—"

"What did you do to my shed?"

But I know what he did. He had one of his work buddies come over during our family therapy and tear it down. He planned this—he planned this whole thing so he could take down my stuff.

All my work.

Gone.

All my prep.

Gone.

My chances of surviving.

Gone.

"I didn't do anything," he says, real quiet. He's crying.

He reaches for me, but I back away and grab my chest because it's thudding hard like *ba-boom, ba-boom, ba-boom.* I'm panting like a wild animal and Dr. Mike is saying *Breathe, Derrick, breathe* and I slouch back in my chair, that black hole in the ceiling staring down at me.

1

"**D**errick."

I sit up in bed, real quick. The hazmat suit is stuck to me like I went swimming. "What's happening?"

"You were yelling," my dad says.

I look at my watch. *3:48 a.m.* I unzip the suit. "So hot."

"Bad dream?"

I shrug.

He sits on the end of the bed. "You remember what it was about?"

I can guess. "No."

"You okay?"

"Gonna get a drink."

I go to the bathroom and down some water. My hair is smashed against my forehead. I definitely smell bad. Good thing I got a couple of these suits, because this one needs to be washed.

My dad comes to the door and says, "You sure you're okay?"

"Yeah."

He stands there a couple more seconds. "I wouldn't just tear it down," he says. "Do you think I would do that to you?"

"I don't know." When we got home from Dr. Mike's, the

shed was still there. But that doesn't mean it will be there tomorrow.

"I'm not going to do that. I wouldn't just do that."

"Okay."

He puts his hand on my shoulder and just leaves it there. I let him and it feels kind of good, his big giant hand, gripping me hard. Not hurting but almost, like if I wanted to get away I'd have some trouble. "Night, son."

I hear a door shut. But it's weird because he went the wrong way—toward the steps. His room is at the back of the house. That's the big one. The master.

I go into the hallway. There's light coming from the guest room, by the steps, and then it cuts out. I hear a bed creaking and then it's quiet.

I look the other way and I'm walking before I know it. I creep to the master bedroom and open the door.

It's neater than a hotel room—nothing out of place. It's like nobody sleeps here. There's a picture of Her on his side of the bed. I can't really see the whole thing in the dark, which is good.

He doesn't sleep here.

How long has this been going on?

I go back to my room and push the earth until I'm sweaty again. I change into a fresh hazmat suit and fall asleep on the floor, holding my go bag.

2

Mrs. Ruth puts two cookies on the guidance office conference table next to me.

"No, thanks. I'm good."

"Everybody likes cookies. Especially mine."

They do look amazing. I eat one.

She leaves and I pretend to do Mrs. Baker's science project. Really I'm checking my phone for the Poop Master 5000 delivery update and looking at my weather app.

Around eleven I get a notification from UPS. *Your package has been delivered.* I jump up and cheer, probably too loud, because Mr. Killroy knocks on the door and opens it.

"Got a visitor," he says.

Brock walks in with two lunch trays. It's pizza and he slides one to me. "It's pizza."

"Yeah."

Mr. Killroy leaves and shuts the door.

We eat pizza and look at each other and then look away real quick. I watch the clock and wonder when he's going to talk, because I'm not planning on it. It was nice of him to buy lunch, but that doesn't make him not a Real Big Jerkface.

"Sorry I threw a big piece of wood at your shed," he says.

"It's fine."

After a while he says, "Tommy has a game today. It's a home game, and it's right after school. You should come."

"Hmm."

"You need to come. You don't even have to stay the whole time. Just for the first half and see him play."

"My toilet just got delivered. I have to go home and set it up in the shed."

"I thought you already got it."

"They didn't have it in the store. I had to get it online."

Brock taps his fingers on the table. "I get that you're messed up because of everything with your mom. That sucks. It really does, and I get that I don't know how bad."

"I can't come."

"You *need* to."

"I *can't*." I slide the tray at him, trying to bang it into his.

He stops it with his big giant arm and just leaves it there, trapped against the table like the million bugs he's murdered. "He's your *best* friend, Dee. Don't you get it?" He gets up and stacks our trays together with a *smack*. "Just come to his game with me, hold a sign, and scream. Witness him with me. This is the coolest thing he's ever done."

"You'll be there."

"He wants *you* there," Brock says. Pretty much yells. "Dude. He worships you. You're bigger and tougher than him and you're always building stuff. And now he's got this one thing and he wants to show you. Are you *getting* this?"

"I can't go," I say, but it's weak and lame. The pizza and cookie are mixing up with all the knots in my gut. I'm over the fifty percent mark now, I can feel it.

I have become a Real Jerk.

Mr. Killroy opens the door. "Time for class, Brock."

He walks to the door, but then comes over to me. He looks me right in the eye and says, "If something happens to Pete, I'm going to bring the thunder."

3

I get off the bus and see the toilet box by the garage when I'm still way far away.

I sprint the rest of the way like I'm in the Olympics. This is it. For real—the actual last thing. In an hour, maybe less, the shed will be done.

I'll be ready.

"Hey!" I shout, because Misty is coming off our front stoop and heading for the package. "Don't touch it."

"I was just watching it, until you came home." Her eyes are red and her hair is sticking out all over the place under her hat.

"I'm here. So you can go." I start dragging the box around the house. It's really heavy, and then it's light all of a sudden.

Misty's picked up the other end.

"You're not my assistant anymore," I say.

She doesn't answer.

Whatever.

We get to the shed and I tear open the box. It's mostly assembled, just the battery has to go in.

"Looks cool," she says.

I get out my screwdriver and open the battery port. "Why are you even here?"

"I was feeling pretty bad about what I did. I acted like the Biggest Jerk Ever."

I slide the lithium rectangle in and screw the plate back on. There's supposed to be a special liner for the toilet, but I don't see it. Misty finds it under a piece of cardboard and hands it to me.

"Shouldn't you be watching the *Princess Diaries* or something?" I ask.

Misty goes to talk but some hair flies in her mouth. She tucks it under her hat. "I watched them all last night."

"Another one for the DONE box," I say. "You could probably do a couple more in the time you're wasting here. Maybe do a back flip."

"I'm sorry—okay?"

"Whatever."

"Okay listen: Have you ever seen those videos of people seeing color for the first time?"

"What?"

Misty shuts the toilet lid so I can't put the liner on. "They make these special glasses that let color-blind people see color. And you know what all the people do at that *exact* moment when they put them on? When they see color? They cry, Derrick."

"What does this even have to do with anything?"

"Just listen." Misty finally gets sick of eating hair and ties a real ponytail with some color band thing on her wrist.

"They cry because it's so incredible. They can't handle it. Get it?"

I check my watch.

"Just google it." She takes off toward her house. "And I am sorry. Okay? People mess up."

I basically break my back trying to lift the toilet in. I move some stuff around and it fits pretty good, right at the foot of the cot. I lie down and let it sink in.

I'm actually done.

I'm ready.

I lie there for a while and stare at the wood plank ceiling. It could happen tonight and I'd be ready. Maybe I should start sleeping here just in case. Could probably run an extension cord out to charge my phone and stuff until the power gets cut by superstorm winds coming east.

I get my phone out and google *colorblind people seeing color*. I watch a couple videos. It's weird and pretty cool actually, seeing them open the glasses and then put them on. As soon as it happens—that exact moment, like Misty said—they cry. I thought one guy wouldn't because he was laughing, but then he started crying.

I hear somebody outside the shed and get up. Tommy's standing there in his soccer stuff. The jersey is super-big on him, and he's got this grass stain down the side of one leg. He's holding a box of mice and Pete is chilling on the ground in his cage.

"Hey," I say.

"Hey."

"Did you guys win?"

"No."

"Oh. Sorry."

"I played pretty good."

"Nice." I feel sort of sick. I look at the ground. At Pete.

"I know the apocalypse isn't till Friday, but I wanted Pete to, like, settle in," he says. "Is that okay?"

I shrug. Nod.

We carry Pete's cage inside and lower him into the snake box. Tommy says goodbye to him and we slide the lid on.

"I'm still trying to find the hinges and lock," I say.

"Cool."

We stare at the box for a while.

"How'd you carry him over here?" I ask. "The cage is pretty heavy."

"Brock helped me. He left."

"Yeah."

We walk outside and stand under the maple tree. Tommy sneezes three times and uses his arm to wipe it. "I was wondering if, like, the apocalypse doesn't happen, if you could come back."

My throat feels like I'm choking. "Hmm."

"You changed," he says. "Like, after your mom and stuff."

He sneezes again. "I thought if we didn't say anything you would just come back. But you didn't."

I say, "Tommy," and he sneezes and then he's sprinting to the sidewalk, faster than I saw him run at practice.

1

"**Y**ou're not taking the bus today." Claudia puts a bunch of stuff in the dishwasher and starts it. "I'm driving you. Okay?"

"Whatever."

"And you might want to wear something else."

"Why?"

"And if anybody at school asks, you're sick."

I watch her. I've barely seen her since Dr. Mike's, and now she's being weird. "What's happening?"

"We're hanging out," she says. "All day."

"Hmm."

"There's only one rule: You have to actually be with me. No waiting in the car."

I think about it. "What if I don't want to?"

She shrugs. "Then you can hang out in that guidance office for another eight hours."

"Hmm." I think some more. "Are we going far? I don't want to be far from the shed."

"Twenty minutes, max." Claudia tilts her head and says, "Deal? You come, you're with me. No bailing."

I wait a couple seconds, and then shrug. "Okay."

I eat some cereal and go out to the shed to check on Pete. He's just lying there looking all snakelike. I think about

Brock bringing the thunder on me and put a crate of MREs on top of the lid so Pete can't sneak out. Should probably find those hinges and a lock.

I walk around to the garage and stop when I see our car.

"Why are the bikes on here?" I ask Claudia.

"It's a real mystery, isn't it? Get in."

She turns left out of our development, the opposite way of school. She's got the pedal pushed seriously to the floor and we're zooming with the other traffic.

"So where are we going?" I ask.

"I'm starving."

I check my watch. Mr. Killroy is probably finishing a biceps workout in his office and waiting for me to come in. "Just tell me where."

"Dee, trust me."

"Aren't you gonna get in trouble for skipping? With colleges and stuff?"

"If you can't cut school two days before the apocalypse, when can you?"

We pass the big Costco and ten furniture stores and the doctor's office we went to as kids. Claudia turns left at a light and then makes a quick right into a tiny parking lot. The neon sign says YUM-YUM DONUTS. It's a small building and looks a hundred years old. My stomach is knotting pretty hard.

"What are we doing here?" I ask.

Claudia shuts the car off and gets some cash out of her purse. "I want some donuts."

"I don't want to be here."

"We made a deal." She turns around and looks at me. "And *I* want to be here—with my brother."

I watch a guy go in, hear the bell on the door ding. I swallow and take big breaths through my nose. Do some fist clenching. "They have donuts other places."

"Not like these," she says.

"Hmm."

"Derrick." She waits till I look at her. "If the world is ending on Friday, this would be a great time to do something really nice for me."

I look at the sign again. Back at her.

"You can do this," she says. "We're just eating donuts."

I get out real slow. The parking lot smells like trash and car exhaust. But it also smells like donuts and it's pretty amazing. It cuts into the dizziness a little and my heart isn't going *ba-boom* real loud in my ears, so that's good. Maybe I can do this.

We walk inside and that bell clangs real loud. *Ding-ding.* There's some seating along the windows, but most people sit at the big bar that runs along the front of the shop. They look at me funny for a second because of the hazmat suit. Claudia heads for two stools right in the middle by the register and we stare at the menu board.

"I'm going to get the glazed," she says. "They're the best."

A short lady with an apron comes over. "What can I get you?"

"Can I have two glazed donuts and a small coffee?" Claudia says. She elbows me.

I look at the menu on the wall but I don't really need to. "Coffee roll and Boston cream."

The lady writes it on her notepad and then checks out my suit for a couple seconds. "Chocolate milk?" she asks.

I nod because chocolate milk sounds exactly right. Like of course I'd get that. "Yeah."

Claudia pays and we eat our donuts as other people come in and talk with the lady in the apron. This big trucker guy in suspenders calls her Maria. I knew that. That's Maria and she knows I get chocolate milk.

"In about two hours," Claudia says, "our blood sugar will crash and we're going to feel like somebody shot us with a tranquilizer dart. Also, you've got chocolate all over your face."

I wipe it with a napkin.

"Still there," she says, and does it for me.

A couple minutes go by. I try not to look around because this is going pretty not horrible and who knows what could make it bad. "Sorry I yelled at you. At Dr. Mike's," I say.

We sip our drinks and listen to people chatting about nothing. She side hugs me for a while and then says, "Isn't it funny that Mom brought us here every Saturday? She would never let us eat crap like this at home."

My head goes up and down, but the whole motion feels a little slow, like the muscles aren't working right. Dizziness is coming back.

"I loved that about Her. She had rules, but built in these little windows where we could totally break them." She wipes glaze off her fingers. "I think that was my favorite thing about Her."

I'm taking in these big wafts of donut shop air to try and keep things steady. Any second now that stupid desert movie is going to kick on, which would really be not good. Like now.

Or now.

"She used to get that thing," Claudia says, and she puts her hand on my arm and grips it tight like *Hey, remember that?* and it sort of pauses everything because I do remember *that thing.*

I feel my head nodding a little and I say, "Peanut butter donut with whipped cream," the same time Claudia does.

She squeezes my arm harder and does this really big laugh that echoes across the whole shop. It lights up something in my chest—something nice and bright and warm, a million times stronger than the Great Red Spot. Her laugh is this incredible magical thing that I haven't heard in forever, with a hundred laughs behind it. I can feel myself smiling too and that makes Claudia laugh harder and now pretty much the whole place is looking at us like *Seriously, what is happening with you two?*

"Oh man," Claudia says when she calms down. "How did She not get diabetes?"

"I don't know."

She checks her watch. "Okay. Time to go."

2

We drive back toward our neighborhood but past it a little, turning up this long road that dumps into another development. Claudia winds through it to get to this big park on the other side.

"My school is like one minute away," I say. "Somebody could see us."

"I'm very concerned. Hear the concern in my voice."

Claudia parks and takes the bikes off the back of the car. I get the helmets. "You doing okay?" she asks.

"I think I could take a nap."

"Dee. I'm serious."

I yawn and stretch. Look around. "I'm trying not to think about it that much."

"You're not freaking out, so that's good."

"Yeah."

We ride slow, Claudia in front. The park has sports fields everywhere. Some are just regular grass fields, these giant open spaces. We stop at one of them and watch a guy fly one of those remote-controlled airplanes. He's pretty good and does a lot of flips and tricks with it, then brings it in for a landing. We keep riding and the sugar rush fades a little because I'm sweating it out. I unzip the hazmat suit to my waist and tie the arms so they don't get stuck in the bike wheel.

Claudia slows at this big bend that overlooks a football field. She lays her bike in the grass and climbs onto some empty bleachers and waves me to follow. It's hot, but at least there's a breeze this high up.

"Did Dr. Mike tell you to do this?" I ask. "Therapy in the wild or something?"

"I'm just riding bikes with my brother."

A cloud goes overhead. For a second it's colder—almost like fall. I look at the field and wonder who put the goalposts in, because they're both majorly sagging.

"Hmm," I say. I'm remembering something. I look at Claudia and she's watching me. "She freaked out at somebody," I say. "Yelling and stuff. But I didn't play football."

"We were just riding bikes. You were in fifth grade, I think. It was a while ago."

That makes sense. "A big guy. He yelled at Her."

"They both yelled at each other."

"Why?"

"We stopped to watch because you were into football." Claudia points to the farthest goalpost. "The guy's son missed the extra point kick and he started yelling at him."

I nod. "Yeah."

"Mom told him to stop, and he told Her to buzz off. Got pretty heated. We rode back and She was shaking, She was so mad. I'd never seen Her like that." Claudia pauses, and I'm watching her close because I remember now too. "She told us that a parent's job was to build their kids up, not tear them down."

My throat's all tight. "Why are we really doing this?"

"Because you act like She didn't even exist." Claudia tucks some hair behind her ears. "And Dee, I really hate it."

"I don't do that."

"*Yes,* you do."

"Like how?"

Claudia holds up one finger. "We can't eat at the kitchen table." She holds up another one. "You won't sit in the front seat because of the Air Force sticker." A third. "I had to beg you to come to the cemetery."

My chest goes *ba-boom* real big. "You don't talk about Her either."

"Because every time I do, you shut down or freak out. I don't want to make you upset."

I put my arms back in the hazmat suit and zip it up. "Maybe I don't want to talk about Her."

"Well, I do. Have you ever thought of that?" Claudia picks at her nails. "You're like dynamite. I tiptoe around you so you don't explode. I do your laundry, I make your food, I drive you to school—and I never, ever make fun of your doomsday stuff."

"Yeah, but you think I'm crazy."

"I have *never* said that. And I do *not* think it."

"Then what?" That sounded like a yell. *Ba-BOOM,* my heart goes real loud. "If you don't think the world is ending, then what does that make me?"

She holds her hands up like *What do you want from me?* "You're busted up, Dee. The same as me. The same as Dad. We're all jumbled up and trying to figure it out. That's what happens when people die—it blows everything up."

The desert movie kicks on like she slammed the PLAY button. But it starts really far along this time with those Humvees super-close to me. A couple more seconds and they'll run me right over.

"Dee. Listen to me."

I pull the hazmat hood up and tighten the strings. Can you contain the Great Red Spot? "Mmhm."

"Mom was awesome. And I miss Her *just as much* as you—but I miss remembering how awesome She was because we're never allowed to talk about Her. Do you get that?"

I pull big breaths through my nose and keep my eyes wide open so that movie doesn't get to the end. "Yeah."

"I'm serious."

"I get it."

I get off the bleachers and push the earth. I'm crushing gravity—I own it. Claudia doesn't stop me, just sits and watches. I hit sixty and keep going, like I just started. At seventy-four my arms give out. I lie on my back and look at the clouds and take big giant breaths that my body actually needs this time. The movie stays paused, so mission accomplished.

Claudia comes and sits next to me. I sit up and she leans her head on my shoulder and I feel her crying.

"I love you, Dee."

"Yeah," I say. "Me too. Sorry."

She sniffles. Then she sniffs me. "You need to wash that thing."

"Yeah."

3

At home, I put on a new hazmat suit and throw the dirty ones in the washer. There's like five bottles of detergent and lots of places to put them and tons of buttons. Claudia comes in and does it for me.

"Thanks," I say.

She leans against the washer. "If you want to just go hang out in the shed, it's fine."

I do. Bad.

But we're T-minus two days away, and I have been sort of a Real Jerk to Claudia lately. "We made a deal," I say.

She looks at me. "Yeah?"

"Yeah," I say. "What's next?"

"You hungry again?"

"I'm always hungry."

She disappears and comes back jangling her keys. "Then get ready to eat at the one place Mom never took us for lunch."

It's a five-minute drive to McDonald's. Claudia blasts the AC but lets me hang my hand out the window, the air pushing it up and down. The radio blares this song I don't even know, but it's good—lots of bass and the guy's voice is kind of relaxing. No buzzing or sweating going on. Maybe Claudia is right—maybe I can do this. Not totally freak out about Her.

We pull into the drive-through line. It's six cars deep and stacking up behind us.

"She hated this place," Claudia says.

I see the memory in my head. "We got it on that trip to the mountains and I threw up the whole weekend. She said it was the McDonald's."

"See: This is progress," Claudia says. "We're talking about Her. This is normal."

"Hmm."

"Don't order too much, because we're getting tacos from your favorite place tonight."

"I can eat tons of both."

We inch forward in line. Claudia taps her fingers on the steering wheel and then points across the street to an Italian restaurant. "We should take Dad back there sometime. She loved it."

"Yeah," I say, and feel myself smiling, because I'm watching us eat there in my head—the guys talking Italian in the back, Her asking to sit outside again on their patio, saying stuff about real pasta and homemade sauce. "Maybe tonight we could—"

It falls off, because I can actually see Her right now, sitting outside at that table she loved, next to a guy who looks like my dad—exactly like my dad.

Is my dad.

They're talking and laughing and She keeps throwing

Her hair to the side, and they're sitting really close, and the food is coming and they talk to the waiter and it's live—it's happening now.

But there's a glitch—something's wrong—something is really not right—because Her hair was brown and always shorter because of the military, but this lady has lots of *red* hair that's like a waterfall on fire. But it's definitely my dad sitting there and that is definitely Her table and now I'm out of the car walking toward the road and Claudia says *Dee* and then starts shouting.

Derrick!

Stop!

I don't look both ways.

I don't go to a crosswalk.

I rage.

There's some traffic, but I don't care because I cannot be contained. I am the Great Red Spot. No one knows how long I have been raging or when I will stop.

A car screeches to a halt and that gets my dad's attention. His eHarmony lunch date swings her head too and her red hair hits him in the face. He pulls his hand back from her. They watch me as I cross the grass. I walk up to the gridiron fence that runs around the outdoor eating area and I'm climbing over.

"Derrick," he says, and his face is like *Just wait just wait.* I think about him walking to the guest room. The empty master. The picture of Her on his nightstand that he never sees. My arms are shaking and my hands are fists, but I actually listen to him—I stop. I wait because maybe he has some explanation for this. Maybe this lady with the red hair is some work friend or a second cousin he never told us about. Maybe she's his therapist and she's really busy, so they're meeting over lunch.

But then she grabs his hand. Holds it like a friend or second cousin or therapist never would. He squeezes back.

And then the Great Red Spot explodes out of me.

I rush him and my fists go *thud-thud-thud* into his chest and neck and face. There's blood and my hands are maybe broken—something's definitely wrong with my right one—but I keep hitting because I am the longest-raging storm in the universe and my fury will be felt. The red-haired lady is screaming and Claudia is here screaming too and somebody tries to pull me off. I'm roaring from the eye of the storm *I hate you I hate you I hate you* and he's not even trying to fight back. He's just turning his face away and taking the hits. I yell and stand over him, wanting him to get up so I can rage for a hundred more years. For a thousand.

Claudia and the eHarmony lunch date kneel next to him. People are spilling out of the restaurant and some waiter is yelling for somebody to call the cops. I look at my hands, and then close my right fist and scream 'cause it hurts so bad.

And then I'm floating away, the road and cars melting into the background. I'm watching myself sprint across the street, through the McDonald's parking lot toward my neighborhood, getting farther and farther away in my head. Back to where I don't need to remember anything, where I should have been all along.

To the shed.

1

The Humvees are going so fast and I'm waving my arms yelling *stop* but they can't hear me. They just keep coming and they'll be here any second and I know what happens when they reach me. A giant black hole is opening up in the sky. It's sucking us all up like a vacuum—me and the Humvees and the people in them. I can see some of their faces. They're blank. They don't get that this is The End. I yell louder.

Bang.

I open my eyes. A tiny streak of light cuts across the room right above me. I lift my hand up to it and see the white gauze I put on last night. I try to make a fist and wince.

Bang.

"What?" I say, sitting up. My head pounds. So sweaty. I need water.

"Just making sure Pete wasn't trying to eat you," Misty says. "You were yelling."

"Go away."

She walks around outside the shed to where the cot is and says, "You're kind of freaking everybody out."

"I'm fine."

"Nope. That is not true."

I switch on my headlamp and unwrap the bandage. My knuckles look like golf balls. I douse my hand with hydrogen peroxide and rewrap it, looser this time. My *Survival Guide Handbook* didn't have a chapter on treating punching-your-dad wounds. I guess the swelling has to go down on its own.

This is not good.

My hand is busted.

I can't do a pushup.

I can't defend myself if Killroy or anybody else tries to break in.

All I can do is lie here and listen to the mice scratching as they wait for Pete to inhale them.

"You should have put in an air conditioner," Misty says. "Turn this thing into a doomsday spa. Getaway at the end of the world."

I guzzle half a bottle of water. "Go. Away."

"Let me in."

"There is zero chance of that happening."

She sits down on the other side of the wall. The plywood creaks as she leans against it. "You hurt him pretty good. His face is all bruised."

"He deserved it. Just leave, okay?"

It's quiet for a while. "Did you use the toilet yet?"

"Seriously, leave."

"Did you?"

Ugh. "No. Kind of."

"I can't hear you."

I scoot closer to the wall. "I went, but I didn't flush it yet."

"Why not?"

"Trying to save the battery."

Misty shifts, and I can feel it through the planks. "Claudia told me what happened. About seeing your dad with his girlfriend. I'm sorry."

Girlfriend.

I make a fist by accident. It hurts so bad I don't say anything for a minute. "Just get out of here. You don't even want to be here."

I hear her stand up and then walk away. Good. But then she's yanking on the steel door, trying to lift it up.

"Stop," I say.

"Worth a shot." She comes back to her wall spot. "Did you watch those videos I told you about? The people seeing color?"

I unzip my hazmat suit to the waist with my left hand. Super-clumsy and not good. "Yeah."

"What did you think?"

"They were okay."

"Just okay?"

I finish the rest of the water bottle. "Aren't you supposed to be in school?"

"I'm boycotting."

"Great."

Her phone dings.

"I'll be back." Then she whispers, "Don't go anywhere."

2

I eat an MRE for lunch. It's just like all the blogs said: not horrible, not amazing, but enough to keep me alive. Watery chicken mixture is the main meal, and some pound cake, plus some weird candy. I'm not even hungry, but I'll need my energy real soon.

I try to do a one-handed pushup, but fall and bang my knee pretty bad. On my phone I check the *Apocalypse Soon!* message boards for updates on the supervolcano. Nothing. I reread the texts from my dad and Claudia all saying pretty much the same thing.

Derrick I'm so sorry.

Derrick please come out.

Derrick I love you.

I try to nap, but it's too hot. Pete must be loving it, that cold-blooded creep, just slithering around in the dark. He probably thinks Tommy sent him to a fancy snake hotel.

I'm dozing off when Misty comes back and says, "I've decided that the world *is* ending tomorrow." She sits back down where she was before. I hear a plastic bag *swish* and smell something amazing. "I want in."

"No." I check my watch. *3:43 p.m.* Just over eight hours to go.

"I've been reading about this volcano. Pretty scary stuff. If it happens, I want to be in there. Open up."

"Never going to happen."

"Okay, fine." She sighs. More plastic bag sounds like she's digging around. The smell is getting stronger now, like it's in the shed with me. Meat something. She starts eating and says, "Mmmm."

"What is that?"

"Oh. This? Nothing."

"Nice try. I have plenty of food."

"Maybe." More eating. Lots of loud chewing and *mmm-mmm* sounds. "But you don't have tacos."

My stomach grumbles. "You made tacos?"

"Nope," she says. "I had my mom drive me to that place up in Quakertown. The one next to that Rita's that closed. You know that place?"

"Ugh," I say because *of course* I know that place. "Fiesta Habanero."

"Did you know that means 'pepper party'?" Misty says. "Great name, because there is a party happening in my mouth with all these amazing flavors."

It's like the whole shed is filled with tacos. My mouth is watering. "I was supposed to go there with Claudia last night."

"I think I heard something about that." She says it with her mouth full. "I got a bunch of tamales too. And some empanadas, but I ate most of those on the ride home."

"So you're having a taco party outside my shed," I say. "That's what's happening."

"Could be happening inside your shed. If you let me in."

I get up and dig through my food bin and find some candy bars I packed for when I got sick of eating MREs. I take a bite and chew really hard, but everything still smells like tacos.

"Don't you want your last meal before the world ends to be incredible?" Misty asks. "I can make that happen. Just open up."

"This is a trick."

"What are you taco-ing about?"

"Ugh."

"Okay, that was bad," she says. "But it's not a trick."

"Is anybody else with you?" I can totally see my dad or Brock trying to body-snatch me away or something as soon as I open up. "Who else is out there?"

"They're all in the kitchen, watching us."

"You swear?"

"I swear on these tacos that nobody is out here with me."

I think about it for another five seconds and then unlock the door. I roll it up and blink in the blinding light. Misty is holding a plastic bag packed with takeout containers. She's got a board game under her other arm. *Monopoly?*

I look past her to my deck and see a tiny crowd all

crammed against the inside of the back slider, watching.

Claudia.

My dad.

Misty's mom.

Misty's sister.

Brock.

Tommy.

"They're worried about you," Misty says. "Brock called his mom to bring a camping tent over."

I shake my head. "Brock thinks I'm a Real Jerk. Probably one hundred percent Real Jerk."

"So maybe he does. But he's not leaving."

I keep my hand on the door in case anybody sneaks out of the house and rushes the shed. "Gimme the tacos."

Misty backs up a step. "This is a package deal."

"What?"

"I am a part of the taco party. Let me hang out with you until midnight. Like a countdown to The End."

"No way."

She turns around. "Have a good night not eating tacos."

"Wait." Ugh. "Why are you doing this? Jeez, Misty—I don't even really know you."

She whips back around and yells, "Stop *saying* that. It's not true." She swings the bag of tacos at me. "And some great neighbor you are, anyway. I almost died last year and you didn't remember it."

That actually stings. "Yeah, well—I was sort of out of it. Sorry."

"I'm sorry too, okay?" Misty shrugs it off.

I start to shake my head. But then I smell tacos. "Fine. But you're leaving at 11:59."

Misty waves to the people inside. I see my dad lean over to her mom and say something and then she nods and says something back to him. His face looks a little puffy and there's definitely some dark circles near his eyes.

"One more thing." Misty walks in and looks around. "Don't lock the door. I'm claustrophobic and it freaks me out."

3

We eat on the floor with the overhead lamp on. Maybe these are the best tacos I've ever had. There's only one empanada left because Misty really did eat most of them on the way home. She lets me have it.

"Is your hand okay?" she asks.

"It's fine."

"Infection would really not be good right now."

"I know."

We put the empty containers back in the plastic bags. Misty sits on Pete's box. I'm on the cot opposite her.

"What's the smell?" she asks.

"Pete."

"He really stinks."

"Yeah."

She looks around. "So this is surviving."

"Yeah."

"Pretty boring."

"Mmhm."

She taps the Monopoly box on the floor between us. "Wanna play?"

"That game takes forever."

"Not with me."

"Why? Do you cheat or something?"

"Play me and you'll find out."

"Fine."

She sits on the ground and takes out the pieces. "No, you can't have the car. I am always the car."

We play, and it's like Misty went to college for Monopoly. She knows the spaces by heart, so every time I roll she's saying "Oh you should buy that," or "Wow that's bad luck," or "I'm going to have hotels on that next time around." She trades anything and everything to get sets and soon I can't roll without landing on her stuff. Then I'm broke and have to sell my properties just to keep playing—but she won't pay the price on the card. She keeps saying "It's only worth what I'll pay for it," and the game ends in me forking over all the railroads for twenty bucks total.

"Holy crap," I say. "You destroyed me."

She's counting her money. "Again?"

It's not as bad the second time, but still pretty bad. I last a couple more times around the board, but that only gives her more time to stack up hotels. Two bad rolls in a row blow things up for me and I surrender.

"You should be in Monopoly competitions," I say.

"Wait—is that a thing?"

"I don't know."

"I'm gonna find out."

We start cleaning up the board and I say, "How'd you get so good?"

"Because being in the hospital is really boring. You don't even know." Misty shivers, like she's shaking off the memory. "I mean, people visit, but most of the time you just lie there. Playing Monopoly against myself helped."

I picture it, see her moving pieces around the board, making crazy bad trades with one part of her brain to destroy the other. See her waiting for a kidney. Or The End. "Was it scary? Waiting for It to maybe happen?"

"Yeah. It was."

I'm looking where the black knot is. I can't even see it 'cause of all the shadows and bins, but I know it's there. I want to take a sledgehammer to it. "Like is it still scary, when you think about it?"

She thinks about it and says, "Yeah, but different."

"What do you mean?"

"It's like those color-blind people, getting their special glasses. I mean, I can really see now—all the stuff there is to do. And it's freaking me out."

"Hmm."

"Think about it." Misty waves her arms around in a big circle. "You can't do it all, and if you do one thing, that means you're not doing something else. And what if that other thing is better? And while you're thinking about that, fifty other things are popping up, and you want to do those too. But they all take time, and there's not enough of it."

"Yeah."

Misty fiddles with the car piece. "I'm really sorry I ditched you to watch the *Princess Diaries*. That was a Real Jerk move."

"It's okay."

We put Monopoly away and open an MRE to eat the dessert part. It's pound cake and Misty eats most of it. I sip water and wonder if she'll still be here when I have to go to the bathroom.

"It's funny," she says. "You keep saying we never hung out, but we've been hanging out a lot where we used to hang out. When we'd hang out."

"Yeah," I say. "Wait—what?"

"The shed." Misty dumps the packet into her mouth to get the last crumbs. "Mostly I'd come find you here because of my dad. Remember? He ran out of gas like every week for his mower and you'd give me some."

Gas.

Her mom said that to me, didn't she?

Stealing your gasoline.

And then I'd spotted the red wagon. Black-and-white tires. The one Misty was always pulling. The kind of wagon you'd carry heavy stuff in.

Like a big gasoline container.

It's dead quiet in the shed—just us breathing. Sweat is dripping off me and I smell something in the air, just barely. Left over from what the shed used to be.

A place we kept the lawn mower.

Gasoline.

I'm remembering. I see Misty walking across the Mitchells' yard toward the shed. She waves and I wave back and then I say something and she laughs, then she's right at the door and talking about her dad.

"You needed gas," I say. "You came over because . . . your dad ran out. You had an empty can. In the wagon."

Misty doesn't move. She's like a statue.

I look over at the steel door, right where we were back then, and say, "You were here?" She's totally still, like she's frozen. Is time freezing? "Oh man. Oh man."

Things are tilting. I slide to the ground and Misty grabs my shoulders, saying *Derrick it's okay* but it is definitely not okay—it's the exact opposite of okay and I hear myself say, "We were here when they came." Hot lines of water fall out of my eyes. Misty keeps saying *Derrick it's okay it's okay Derrick* and I hear myself make this weird moaning sound. "You were here," I say, and she's nodding and then I say, "You saw them—did you see them?"

Because now *I* see them—two guys in blue uniforms and they're standing on the deck and my dad is there and Claudia is there and I'm in the shed, watching. Misty's here

254

with the empty gas can and the red wagon, old but in good shape with big black-and-white tires, and I'm wondering why they're all looking at me, but I *know* why—everybody knows why they come. My dad calls for me. *Son.* But his voice isn't right. None of it's right, but I go anyway, across the grass where Claudia is crying and the military guys look all serious and my dad says *We should go inside.* The one military guy's lips are moving and I hear it in my head.

Deepest regret.

Killed in action.

Improvised explosive device.

I try to get up but fall and then scramble past Misty, shoving the snake box hard to one side and kicking some bins to the other because something else is here too—something important and wrong that I have to get to because it's been here with me all along. I fumble for my headlamp and switch it on so I can stare at the plank.

At the black knot of wood.

I scream at it and go to punch it with my busted hand but Misty grabs my arm and so I end up sort of falling into it, my head an inch from it, face-to-face. I put my good hand against it, trying to cover it up because now I can see.

Now I remember.

4

I don't know how long I've been crying.

I look at my watch.

8:21 p.m.

A long time.

I take my hand off the plank. Misty gives me some water and I gulp it down.

"I sat here," I say, and it comes out all hoarse. "After they told us. I think I was dazed or something."

"One of the Air Force guys told your dad you were in shock." Misty's sitting Tommy-close, but it's not annoying.

"You were still here?"

She nods. "Until my mom made me come home."

I unzip the hazmat suit. My shirt is totally soaked. "They said She was on her way to a military base in Iraq. There was a bomb on the road. They said She died right away."

"I'm so sorry."

"Like She was just gone, you know? Like we all talked to Her a couple days before, but then She was gone." I wipe my nose. "And my dad—I just don't get it. How can he keep going when She's gone?"

Misty just nods.

"Oh man." I lie down and shut my eyes. I should be terrified because The End is basically here. Hours away.

But I feel kinda good, like that Jupiter storm probably feels when it's taking a break. Or maybe when it's finally done.

"Maybe you could stay," I say. "Like before."

"Yeah."

Misty starts humming this song, and I'm asleep in seconds.

1

"**D**errick."

I forget where I'm at for a second.

"Derrick," Misty whispers. "Wake up."

I start to sit up, but she's holding me down.

"Don't move."

"Why are we whispering?"

I hear her swallow. "Pete got out."

"What?"

"I got up to get some more water, and I saw the top of his box was off."

My brain is scrambled. "But he's in a glass cage inside the box."

"I think it broke," she whispers. "When you moved it. Something broke."

"How do you know?"

She puts an index finger to her lips and points up. My heart pounds. I don't see anything until she moves my head-lamp beam to the right.

"*Ah*—" I start to scream, but Misty clamps her hand on my mouth.

All five feet of Pete is hanging from one of my rafter hooks.

"*Shhhhhhh,*" she says.

I nod real quick. She lets go and I whisper, "Oh man. He thinks I'm Tommy. He wants to eat me."

"We need to go. Real slow. Really, really slow. Okay?"

"Yeah."

Misty gets to her knees. It takes me longer since I'm on my back, but finally we're in crawling position.

"You first," I say, and she's on her way. Every scrape and bump and scuff seems like dynamite going off, but we're getting there. Just a couple more feet.

Thunk.

We freeze.

"What was that?" Misty hisses.

I swing my beam up and—

"Oh crap," I say. "He's not there."

"Where is he?"

"Forget it! Just go—*go!*" and I jump up to run the last five feet. Only Misty is still going with the crawling plan, so I trip over her and go flying, shoulder first into the door. This horrible *crunch* sound rips through the shed.

"Oh man," I say. "Sorry. Are you okay?"

"Yeah. Are you?"

"I think so." I rotate my shoulder, then swing the light across the shed. No sign of Pete. *Crap.*

I grip the steel door handle with my good hand and pull.

It won't budge.

"Hurry," Misty says.

"I'm trying." I pull harder, but it only goes an inch. "What the—"

And then my light hits it: the door track.

It's bent.

"No no no," I say, trying to yank it up again, but it's twisted right above the wheel. *Crap.* I swing my beam around and scan for my toolbox. There—other side of the door. I dig through it but *crap crap crap* it's not in here. My crowbar, to wedge the track back in place. I left it in the garage.

No.

"What's wrong?" Misty asks.

"The track is busted." I scoot over and try to shove it back into place. "Maybe I can—"

"Shhhh."

I freeze. Listen. Shine my light around.

Pete is coiled a couple feet away, right in the middle of the shed. His tongue is going in and out.

"Derrick," Misty says. "I am starting to freak out."

The fear in her voice kicks mine out for a second and I mentally scan my survival book. There's stuff about snake bites, but nothing about avoiding a constrictor you brought into your own shed.

Crap.

I swing the light around the room, looking for things to fend off Pete with when I spot it—the mice box. It's on top of the Poop Master 5000.

Mice.

Poop Master 5000.

Pete.

Bingo.

"Okay, listen. Listen." I reach over Misty and unhook the fire extinguisher from the wall. "If he comes at you, poke him back with this."

"What? Will that work?"

"I don't know."

"What are you gonna do?"

"No time." I dig in the bin next to her and pull out a bigger flashlight. "Just keep this on him so we know where he is."

"Okay."

I turn off my headlamp and inch toward the left wall. Can snakes see in the dark? I don't know. I move slow, stopping when my legs bump into the cot. I crawl onto it. Pete's coiled up, still just watching us. Good Pete. Stay.

I make it to the other side of the cot and lift up the toilet seat. Pete doesn't move. "Good boy," I say, and Misty says, "Why are you talking to him?" but I'm all adrenaline now. I pick up the mice box and start to open it. They go crazy.

"Watch out!" Misty says, and I see Pete slither toward

me and then *clang*—something goes flying by his head. She chucked the fire extinguisher at him. "He's coming for you!"

I'm frozen, watching him slither onto the cot, his gross reptile skin all wet and nasty on my sleeping bag.

"Derrick—move!" Misty shouts.

I unfreeze.

I dump the mice into the Poop Master 5000. Then I leap off the cot just as Pete sticks his head into the toilet after them. He's going nuts in there, snapping and thrashing like a snake version of bobbing for apples, his back half still slapping around on my sleeping bag. A few mice make it out and I think *Good for them* but that means Pete could slither out too and he's gonna be pretty mad that I shoved him in a dark hole that has some of my pee in it.

Time to finish this.

I grab the sleeping bag with my good hand and fling the rest of him into the toilet. Then I slam the lid shut and sit on it.

"Whaaaaaat!" Misty shrieks. *"That was amazing! Derrick!"*

"Oh man."

Misty keeps pumping me on the back yelling about me almost dying by snake attack. I'm feeling really tired all of a sudden. "It was my fault he got out. I never put the hinges or lock on and then I busted his cage open. Man, that was close."

"I thought he had you."

I take a couple breaths. "Grab that bin right there with all the batteries."

Misty hauls it over and I put it on the toilet seat to keep it down. No noise from Pete.

"So what do we do with him?" she asks.

"We flush him."

"Why not just leave him?"

"I can't. Brock is going to bring the thunder if he finds out this happened." Ugh. He was right. About so many things. "It won't hurt him—it's a dry flush. It will just seal up the bag and then I'll lift him back into the box."

"So how do we flush it?"

I reach around and feel for the button. "Kinda glad we get to try this, anyway. It was pretty expensive."

"Yeah. Okay—let's bag this reptile."

I press the button.

It doesn't make any sound at first, and then it makes a ton of sounds—a soft hum that kind of vibrates the shed floor. Then it's a sort of motor sound—that's probably the bag part cinching up. Now it's a gear grinding, and it doesn't sound good. It's getting louder and louder and Misty is saying, "Should it be making that sound?" and then it shuts off.

"Maybe he clogged it," I say.

"How do you clog a dry toilet?"

There's a weird cloud of dust wafting up from the back,

and my headlamp is getting all these particles in the beam, and then I realize it's not dust.

It's smoke.

"Oh man," I say.

"What is that?"

There's a burst of something, and a tiny orange flame kicks up around the back edge. I say, "Fire," but it's not that loud, and Misty says "What?" And now I'm screaming.

Fire!

2

I stumble back and knock Misty over.

Fire.

Fire.

Fire.

I yank her up and she says, "You need to get that door open."

I lunge for it and yank harder with my left hand, but it's not enough.

It won't budge.

I bang on it and scream and then kick it as hard as I can to make noise—somebody has to hear.

Please.

Somebody.

I keep kicking and yelling and then hear somebody outside yell, *"Derrick!"*

"Dad!" I scream back. "There's a fire—and the door is stuck!"

He's yanking too—I can see his fingers hooked under the bottom and now he's yelling, "Grab it!" and there's other hands joining him. Maybe like eight hands and they're all lifting, but the track is so bent it doesn't matter.

"Get my crowbar!" I yell to them. "In the garage."

"Hurry!" Misty shouts.

Fire.

Fire.

Fire.

I rip open the gas mask bin, throwing one to Misty and then me.

"Derrick!" she yells, sort of muffled in the mask, pointing at the corner where that little flame has jumped to my cot. I grab some water bottles, but it gets to my sleeping bag, which goes up like paper.

Fire.

Fire.

Fire.

Then I see it—the fire extinguisher, lying on the floor. I crawl on my belly for it and feel the heat warm my face. I slink back to the door and fumble with the plastic cord, tear it off, and then aim at the cot. I've read the directions a hundred times. I know exactly how to use this.

Grip handle.

Point toward flame.

Depress indicator button.

The extinguisher shakes in my grip as the nozzle flies off the end like a bullet. This weird foam oozes out maybe two inches. I keep pressing, looking at it through the smoke to make sure I'm doing it right.

Nothing's coming out.

It's broken.

Misty screams inside her mask. Now she's banging on the door, fists pounding, and I keep pressing the stupid button. The flames are growing. I chuck the busted extinguisher and slide the snake box between us and the flames. I stack bins on top to block the heat.

"Derrick!" my dad yells, and a crowbar slides under. I grab it and try to bend the track back—but it's so twisted from all the yanking.

I rip my mask off and yell, "It's broken. *Dad.*"

Fire.

Fire.

Fire.

I cough and choke and put my mask back on. The flames are roaring now—burning down the wall of stuff between us. Misty is freaking out and rips her mask off— she's hyperventilating. I'm trying to make her put it back on and screaming *I'm sorry I'm sorry* but she's in full panic mode and way stronger than me. She can't get air and now she's sliding to the floor. I grab her shoulders and yell, but she's limp. I put the mask back on her face and try to think, but the terror is like a black hole. Like that knot of wood—a sign that we've finally arrived.

The End.

Because of me.

THUNK.

THUNK.

THUNK.

It's like the shed is exploding.

"Get away from the wall!" my dad yells.

THUNK.

THUNK.

THUNK.

A silver piece of metal smashes through the plank where my head was five seconds ago. It pulls out and crashes through again and again and again as he hacks at the shed wall.

THUNK.

THUNK.

THUNK goes his ax. There's a huge *craaaaaaaaaaaaack* as a hole opens up. I see tree trunk arms pulling back pieces of the planks to make it wider because Brock is here—and when he comes, he brings the thunder. Tommy is here too, digging at jagged splinters, and my dad comes into view with the ax yelling, *"Son!"* like he did That Day.

"Take Misty!" I pick her up and don't even feel my busted hand. I think she's mumbling something—she's still here. My muscles go into overdrive and I hoist her headfirst through the hole to a bunch of waiting hands.

I jump and yell. Something just bit my calf.

Fire.

My leg is on fire.

I whack at it with my hands, but it's not working, so I

wriggle out of the suit. My leg is this weird mix of red and black. Shouldn't that hurt?

"Come on!" my dad yells.

I shove my arms through and they start pulling, but the shards are digging into me big-time. *"It's too small!"* I yell, and sink back inside. I see my dad's face in the firelight, all wide eyes and he's jacked up on adrenaline and ready to do something crazy.

"Get out of the way!" he yells. He drops the ax and runs back a couple steps and now he's running full speed at the shed and lifting his foot like a front kick. *"Move!"* he screams, and I cram myself into the corner just as the heel of his big shoe slams through the planks and rips the hole wide open. His whole body launches through like the Hulk—he's almost in the fire and I try to pull him back, but he's shoving me outside.

I suck in cool air as people carry me away. I'm screaming *Dad Dad Dad* but they don't listen. The shed is so bright, all of it on fire. I can't see him. Fire engines honk everywhere. Somebody is streaking at the shed—Claudia—but a firefighter bear-hugs her, lifting her off the ground. Another firefighter gets there, and then another, and then they're pulling on something and finally my dad topples out. They drag him toward me and suddenly there's giant streams of water dousing the fire. I'm coughing and crying and scanning the lawn for Misty.

And then I see her.

On the ground, by the deck.

An EMT pushing on her chest with both hands.

22 **SEPTEMBER**

SATURDAY

0 **1** **AFTER THE END**

DAYS

1

My eyes open and I'm staring at a ceiling. It's tiled like the one in Mr. Killroy's office, but no watermark. There's beeping sounds, but it's mostly quiet. Light is coming in a window and I feel pretty relaxed.

Then it all comes back.

Fire.

Fire.

Fire.

I try to sit up, but my head is so heavy. I fall right back. I yell, but it's a raspy version of *"Misty."* I start to pull all these wires out, but I'm so tired I just flail at the machines and more stuff beeps.

"Look who's up," a nurse says. She leans over me to reconnect the wires. Her ID says *Mary* and she looks older and pretty tough.

"Dee," somebody says.

I see Claudia in a big hospital chair near the bed. Her hair is everywhere and her eyes are puffy. She comes over and hugs me for probably five minutes.

"Misty," I croak.

"She's okay. Smoke inhalation, like you and Dad."

"Where is she?"

"Her parents transferred her down to Children's Hospital in Philly because that's where all her transplant doctors are."

"Oh man." My eyes burn.

She hugs me again. "She's gonna be fine."

"You're sure she's okay?"

"Brynn's been texting me nonstop. She's totally okay."

I lie back on the pillow. "Dad?"

"He's got some deep cuts on his right leg and stomach, but nothing major."

"Oh man, he must've got stabbed by those plank shards."

"He's tough, Dee. He can take it." She grips my good hand pretty hard. "You got it the worst."

"What?"

Claudia pulls the covers down so I can see my left leg. It's wrapped in gauze from ankle to knee. "Second-degree burns, almost third they said. Plus your hand."

I look at the white cast that goes halfway up my right arm. "I thought it was maybe broken."

Claudia reaches over and rotates the cast. Somebody scrawled a message in big black marker that says *This arm pushed the earth out of orbit.*

"Brock said you'd get it," she says.

Brock.

Tommy.

"Pete," I say. "Oh no."

"You may *not* bring that snake in here," Nurse Mary barks outside the room. "It's too big."

But Tommy is already in the room, a giant green stuffed animal snake coiled around his body. Brock is right behind him. They both crash into my bed for this group hug and Tommy says, "You saved him."

"I what?"

"Witness me witnessing your genius," Brock says. "Vacuum-sealing a snake inside a fireproof crapper with just enough oxygen so he doesn't suffocate and just enough urine so he doesn't dry out."

I just stare. "Guys."

"I can't believe you, like, picked him up," Tommy says. "Even I'm scared to do that."

Then I start laughing. It hurts my lungs so bad, but I can't stop. It turns to coughing and Nurse Mary comes in to check on me, but I wave her off. "Oh man," I say, wiping my eyes. *"Oh man."*

I tell them the story. They go insane all over again. Brock makes me reenact it using the stuffed snake and Claudia laughs so hard she almost passes out. Nurse Mary keeps coming in and telling everybody to keep it down because *Derrick needs to rest.* They say sorry and pull chairs up to the bed. Claudia sits on the window ledge and takes a couple pictures of us with her phone.

"We tried to come yesterday," Tommy says. "They wouldn't let us."

"Yesterday." I look around for my watch but can't find it. "Wait, what day is it?"

"It's Saturday afternoon, Dee," Claudia says.

Saturday.

I swallow real hard and wait for the buzzing in my hands to get going.

But it doesn't.

"It didn't blow," I say.

Tommy shakes his head.

"So we're okay. We're good."

"We're good," Claudia says.

"But a couple of Yellowstone campers are not okay," Brock says. "They fell into a hot spring and had to get airlifted to a hospital."

"Hmm," I say.

Tommy leans in close. I almost hug him. "It's, like, kind of funny what happened: You were worried about a fire really far away, but then you burned your shed down."

"You were supposed to wait on that joke," Brock tells him.

"Guys." My throat is all tight. "Thanks. For coming to get me."

Tommy wraps me up in a snake hug. "You're back."

I hug him hard and say, "Yeah."

2

Nurse Susan, who's younger and funnier than Nurse Mary, wakes me up for dinner. I inhale hospital meat loaf, which is pretty good after those MREs. Tommy's mom trades places with Claudia, who goes home to shower and change. There's a TV with all the channels and I find ESPN3, but instead of watching Norwegian dudes flipping monster truck tires I just stare out the window.

I made it past The End.

I survived.

But not really.

I was saved—my dad saved me. Sort of a big difference.

Nurse Susan changes my leg bandage, which hurts like crazy, and then helps me walk to the bathroom. I sit down, but she doesn't leave.

"I'm good," I say.

"Not if you faint and crack your head," she says. "I might just leave you on the floor if that happens. Less paperwork."

When I'm done, I try to stand up, but things get all woozy. She grabs me under the arm and lowers me back down. "Your body's been through a lot. Give it a second."

I take a couple deep breaths. She's watching me really close, her face like *I've got a secret.* "What?"

"Your friends didn't tell you?"

"Tell me what?"

"We've had at least five reporters show up," she says. "One tried to sneak in, said he was your cousin."

"Why? Am I in trouble?"

"No—I don't think so."

"What did they want?"

"Wanted to talk to you about your dad. For saving you and that girl."

My eyes burn again. "Oh man."

"What's wrong?"

I shake my head. Hold up my cast. "I got this because I punched him so hard I broke my hand. And then he saves me. Like"—and I'm totally crying now, on a toilet, with a stranger, still sort of woozy—"what kind of person does that? Goes into a burning shed for somebody who did that to them?"

She sort of laughs and says, "A parent. That's who."

"You don't know the rest. I've been the worst—the actual worst. I don't think you can even understand. I've been a Real Jerk, one hundred and ten percent Jerk Material. If you googled *Jerk Face*, you'd find books about me."

She hands me some toilet paper to wipe my face. "My oldest son totaled my car because he was texting. Cost me fifteen thousand dollars."

"Did you forgive him?"

"Of course."

"Like, did you really?"

"He's my son," she says, and I think about my dad, screaming at me from outside the shed, fire raging at my back. Him realizing there's only one way I get out.

Son.

Son.

Son.

If he jumps into the flames.

Right to the edge of The End.

"Maybe we could get a wheelchair," I say.

3

I'm staring at his eHarmony girlfriend.

She doesn't look so mean now, up close. She looks like a regular lady: red hair. Tallish. Younger than my mom, I think. She's reading a book, sitting next to his hospital bed.

"What's her name again?" I whisper.

"Ellen," Nurse Susan says.

"Okay."

She wheels me in. Ellen gets up from the chair and walks toward me. Stops a couple feet away. "Derrick. How are you feeling?"

"Okay."

"We just came up to see Luke," Nurse Susan says.

"They took him to run another test," Ellen says. "He should be done soon."

"We can come back," I say, but Susan just leaves me. I fidget in the wheelchair and Ellen stands there. There's beeping coming from the other guy's bed near the door, but he's sleeping.

Finally she says, "I'm so sorry, Derrick."

"Yeah." Then I ask, "For what?"

"That you had to find out about me like you did."

"Oh. Right."

"Your dad was waiting to introduce me to you and Claudia until he was sure it was serious, I think."

I fidget some more. "So is it?"

She looks around the hospital room. "Feels pretty serious to me."

Hmm. She's kinda funny. "I thought he was dating a bunch of women."

She laughs, and it's sort of relaxing. Her eyes are all lit up and I keep thinking, *I'm talking to the lady who is trying to take Her place.*

"I'm fairly certain he's not," she says.

"Hmm." It's awkward again. "So do you work with him or something?"

"No. I sell houses."

"You're a realtor," I say, and think of a joke from before. Something She used to say.

"I know. Your mom thought we were a bunch of scam artists."

"Yeah."

"Your dad told me that on our second date."

I pick at the edges of the super-thin gown they gave me. "You don't have any kids, do you? That would be weird, I think."

She laughs again. "Sorry. I have a five-year-old son. But he's not too weird."

"What's his name?"

"Max."

"Hmm."

"We named him after his dad," Ellen says, and just in the tone I can feel It—like when Claudia talks about Her. "He died in a car accident when Max was two."

"Oh," I say. "That sucks."

"Yeah. It does." She looks behind me at something and says, "But the thing about life is, it keeps moving. And it's crammed with surprises."

There's a noise behind us and a new nurse says, "And who's this?"

Ellen turns my chair around to face my dad. He says, "Bonnie, this is my son, Derrick."

I wave at her, and she gives me a face like *Oh, so you're the famous Derrick.* She checks a couple of things on her chart and then says, "If I leave you two alone, are you going to fight?"

I shake my head. Look at the floor. She and Ellen go outside, so it's just me and my dad, our wheelchairs a couple feet apart.

"How's your leg?" my dad asks.

"Okay, I think. I'm on some medicine, but it hurts pretty bad."

"And your hand?"

"It's okay."

I'm having a hard time looking at him because his banged-up face makes me feel horrible. I keep flicking my eyes to him, and then to the ground, and then to his leg—bandaged from the ankle up like he fought some barbed wire. Parts of his arms are wrapped up too.

I slump in the wheelchair and cover my face with my hands. I see his wheels rolling up next to me. Our chairs bump against each other and then he's awkwardly side hugging me, and I'm leaning into his giant arms, sobbing like a little kid.

"Dad," I say, but it's all messed up and slobbery. "Dad."

He pulls me closer with both hands. I stay like that for a while, trying to get in an *I'm sorry* and he says *It's okay* and I realize that this is the first time since It happened that we've hugged. I wonder if he missed it, which is something you don't think about with your dad. But I think maybe he did miss it, and I did too—missed it more than I could know until actually doing it again.

I wipe my face and say, "Ellen seems pretty nice."

"Yeah. She is."

"You know she's a realtor, right?"

We share a grin, but he's frowning now. "Derrick. I should have told you."

"No—I'm sorry. The hitting and stuff. And for all the other stuff." I clear my throat, giving the eye-burning a second to go away. "Dad—I just really, like I was so mad at you for going out with those women, and then when I saw you with her, I just like . . . exploded because it was at Mom's favorite place and—"

"I know. I know." He shakes his head. "I wanted to tell you, but—I just didn't want to make things worse for you. And I was still figuring it out myself."

"Yeah."

We sit in silence for a little while. Nurse Bonnie comes in and checks on the guy in the other bed, then leaves.

"So you met her online," I say, "eHarmony or something."

"I was on those sites for a while. Went on a few dates." He shrugs. "Didn't work."

"Hmm."

He sits up, and his face brightens like he's talking about something epic. "Your mom . . . She was *incredible*. It wasn't even about the other women, Derrick—I'm sure they were all perfectly nice. It's what they *weren't*." He's gripping my arm now with his giant hand, and I put my casted hand over it, because he's about to get there—to the thing I've been dying to hear. "There's not another version of Her out there."

I sniffle. "Like I thought maybe you wanted to forget about Her. I thought you were just leaving Her back there."

"*Impossible*. And also the problem." His shoulders sag. "I

gave up all that Internet stuff and started going to a grief support group. Other guys who lost close family."

"What? When?"

"At night, after dinner."

"Hmm. I thought you were going on dates."

He laughs. "Not usually. But I did meet Ellen through one of the guys in the group."

That makes sense. "She told me about her husband."

"She tell you about Max?"

"Uh-huh."

"I've only met him twice; Ellen is very protective of men entering his life." He looks at me, his face like *I am so sorry*. "This is not how you should've found out. I messed this up, bad. I messed up in a lot of ways."

"It's okay." I'm starting to get really tired, probably totally dehydrated from all the crying. "Dad."

"Yeah."

"Stuff has been, um—things have been weird, like in my head. Stuff about Mom."

And then I tell him what I remembered about That Day. I let it out in stutters and it's easier the second time. Telling it again is like reopening that valve and even more pressure comes off my chest and it's incredible. Probably Dr. Mike would pay big bucks to just watch this go down, but too bad, because this isn't for him—it's for me. For my dad, and Claudia. For Brock and Tommy and Misty.

And Her.

Dr. Laura Waters.

Major, United States Air Force.

Mom.

28 SEPTEMBER FRIDAY

07 DAYS AFTER THE END

"**R**ed means I love you," Tommy says.

I scan the other flower options inside the little produce shop. "What color is just friends? But could also say *Sorry I almost burnt you alive?*"

"Witness you being funny again." Brock picks out a bunch of white flowers. "This is what you want."

"I don't even know if she likes flowers," I say.

"She'll like your other gift more. So, like, it's fine," Tommy says.

Claudia honks the horn outside and we hustle to the counter and pay.

"I could pick out a prom dress faster than you ladies in there," she says when we climb back in the Subaru.

"Yeah," I say. "But you'd be sitting at home in it because nobody wants to go with you."

"Boom, roasted," Brock says. He fist-bumps with Tommy. "He is so back."

There's a ton of random traffic getting into the city, so we don't get to Children's Hospital of Philadelphia until five. Claudia parks, and we go through some crazy security to get inside the building. I lead the way to the elevators, basically speed-walking, flowers in one hand and a gift-wrapped rectangular box under my arm. We get off at the seventh floor and I slide around a corner, checking directions, and then running back when I make a wrong turn. My heart is racing and the flowers are bouncing and I can feel butterflies doing great epic battle in my gut.

"That's it," I say, pointing to a sign that says PEDIATRIC ICU.

I go to a big check-in desk. This real serious guy behind a computer watches us all run up and says, "There is no running on this floor."

"Sorry," I say. "We're here to see Misty Knoll."

He types some stuff on his computer.

"Who?"

"Mercedes Knoll."

He squints at the screen. "I have a Mercedes Knoll here, yes. Room fifteen."

"Great."

"Please do not run," he says, but all of us are already running.

The door for Room 15 is open and sun is shining through it from some big window and now it hits me that for all my flowers and presents and racing to get here, I'm not sure what I'm going to say. I sort of slide to a stop, and my sandal gets caught on my foot and I bang into the door frame with my burnt leg.

"Ah," I say, and inside the room Brynn looks up. I can only see Misty's lower half under a blanket on the bed. I back away.

Tommy and Brock rush past me, waving big signs that say SHE ALMOST DIED (AGAIN) BUT NOW IS TOTALLY FINE (AGAIN). I stand just outside the doorway, shifting back and forth, ignoring the burning leg and realizing that I might actually puke from nervousness.

"You got this," Claudia whispers behind me.

"What if she doesn't want me here? What if she doesn't want to be friends because of—you know."

"That might happen." Claudia pushes me forward a little. "But maybe not."

I go in the room. Misty looks thinner and whiter-faced than usual, but pretty healthy. Her wavy ponytail is slung over one shoulder and she's smiling as Brock and Tommy act out their version of Pete almost eating us alive. She sees me and the smile turns into the Stare. I look at the floor. It's really quiet and awkward. I walk to the side of her bed holding out the white flowers and she takes them, smells them, then plays with the plastic wrapping.

Tommy says, "White is, like, the friend color."

Brock shoves him. Misty smells them again. It's like a year goes by before she says, "I hate—" but then she coughs, and Brynn hands her a cup of water. My stomach is churning and I start to back up, but Claudia pushes me forward.

"I hate the food here," Misty says. "Did you bring anything?"

Claudia hands her a plastic bag with a couple of those foam takeout containers. "Derrick's treat."

She smiles and pulls one out and starts inhaling the tacos I got her. She keeps looking at me real quick and I keep looking at the floor, and it's getting pretty obvious that I'm the one making this all super-uncomfortable.

"They said I can go home soon," Misty says.

"Sunday," Brynn tells us. "Doctors just want to make sure all is good."

"How's your dad?" Misty asks Claudia.

"All stitched up. Almost back at work."

"I was hoping he'd come with you so I could thank him."

"You mean," Brock says, pulling up something on his phone, "so you could take a selfie with local hero Luke Waters?"

Everybody laughs as he waves around the headline *Super-human Dad Rescues Teens*. It's got a picture of my dad from high school when he kind of looked like Clark Kent, which probably helped the story go viral. There was still a camera guy trolling our street when we left for school this morning.

"Tell him I'm coming over when I get home," Misty says. "Tell him. Okay?"

"Will do." Claudia gives her a hug, then says to everybody else, "There's a Starbucks on the bottom floor of this place and I'm buying. Let's go."

They all get the hint and head out. It's just me and Misty.

"So," I say.

"So."

Misty pushes up a little in her bed and points to a chair right next to the bed. I sit down. She finishes the second container of tacos pretty fast.

"This was the room," she says.

"What?"

"My room when I was sick, waiting for my kidney."

"Oh man," I say. "Wow."

"I mean, what are the odds that this room was open when they transferred me?"

"Pretty low, I guess."

"Probably one in a billion."

"One in a billion billion."

Misty motions for me to scoot closer. She grabs a black Sharpie from her side table and scrawls four lines on my cast, then a fifth diagonal one across them, and then two more. "Seven days after."

"Hmm."

"What are all your people on the blog saying about the volcano?"

I shrug. "My dad canceled the subscription. And actually, I don't want to get back on it."

"I think you should keep not getting on it," she says. "I think that never again, for the rest of your life, should you go on it."

"Yeah."

Misty caps the marker and leans back. "I can't decide if I should hug you or punch you. I mean, you saved me from dying, but also you almost killed me."

"That's true."

"I'm kidding."

"No, but really—Misty, I'm so sorry."

"Duh."

"No. Listen. All my plans, my stuff—that fire extinguisher. The snake box. That *stupid* door." Eyes burning. Throat tight. "Everything failed. It was like you said that one day, when you were at the shed."

"What did I say?"

"That's the sort of stuff that would happen if the world was ending."

"That sounds like something I'd say."

I shake my head. "Misty. You were trying to help me and then I almost—after you just got better—ah. I can't even really handle it still."

"You didn't force me to be there," she says.

"Yeah."

"But I forgive you."

She grabs a stack of index cards from her side table. Some have writing on them, but most are blank. I watch her write *Escaped a burning shed*. On the next one she writes *Avoided getting eaten by a hungry and very upset ball python named Pete*.

She thinks for a little and then writes *Had CPR done to me* and I wince a little.

"So you're still doing the cards," I say.

"Kind of." Misty taps her pen on another empty one, then writes *Helped a friend stop being a jerk.* "That's you."

"Yeah."

She thinks for a little before writing *Helped a friend stop being so sad.* She's pressing harder now, the marker bleeding a little into the card, making the words stand out.

Got really nice flowers from Derrick as an apology for almost killing me.

Ate the world's best tacos (again).

Finally figured out what SMH means in a text.

"Brynn told me today," she says. "It means 'shaking my head.' Isn't that stupid?"

"Yeah. It is." I notice she's going back to each card and writing the date on them. "So it's stuff you've done? Not stuff you want to do?"

"Yeah. I'm trying it out. Keeping track in the reverse order so I don't freak out thinking about all the stuff I have to do still."

"Is it working?"

"I don't know." She shrugs. "We'll see. I mean, I'm just getting started. Again."

We both smirk.

"I got you a present," I say.

I give her the box and she unwraps it. The wires on her hands get in the way, so it's slow, but she sees what it is about halfway through and laughs, her choking donkey sounds so loud it draws in some traffic from the hall.

"How is this even a thing?" she asks.

"I know."

"I'm still going to crush you."

"We'll see."

She smooths the covers so the bed is nice and flat. We set up the board and play five rounds of *Monopoly: Apocalypse Edition.*

"If the sign is a clue, this is going to be incredible," Misty says.

Tommy gawks out the Subaru window as we pull into the Brazilian Steakhouse near the old air base. "Kelly made me eat Tums before I left."

"Not a bad idea," Claudia says.

"Just remember," Brock tells us. "You need to pace yourself. There will always be another waiter with more meat. Don't get sucked into the frenzy."

Claudia parks and the five of us pile out. It's freezing and I throw on this wool hat my mom got me the Christmas before She died. My dad's truck pulls in and I wave. Ellen's with him, and it's not totally weird anymore. It's still a little weird, but it's also kind of good. She's not my mom, but she gets it.

They park and Ellen opens the rear cab door so Max can get out. He stays pretty close to her until he sees me, and then runs over. We high-five and do the bodybuilder flex pose we usually do when we watch Ukrainian guys pull buses on ESPN3. We make snowballs out of the leftover stuff from last week's storm and peg a light pole until Misty's parents and Brynn show up.

"I'm so hungry," I say as we walk inside. "I didn't eat all

day just for this."

"Pace. Yourself," Brock says.

My dad gives the hostess our name and we follow her to this back room that's kind of separate. It has a big long table with some regular chairs, but on the ends are these giant ones that look like thrones.

"And where are the birthday girls?" the lady asks. Misty shoots her hand up and marches to one of the thrones.

I look down at the second one. The one that will be empty. "The other one isn't gonna make it," I say.

"Oh. I'm sorry to hear that."

"Yeah. It sucks." I clear my throat. "But we're dealing with it."

We all get seats and the waiter points to this salad bar that is bigger than our entire downstairs and then these guys bring out platters of meat. Brock keeps telling people to take it easy, but then forks like six pieces of steak onto his plate and says *I don't even care* and eats with both hands. I see Misty doing the same, grinning as sauce gets all over her face. Tommy close talks with Max about snakes. Brynn and Claudia show each other pictures on their phones and probably talk about college.

"Hey," my dad says. "You doing okay?"

We're across from each other, on either side of the empty throne.

"Yeah," I say. "I'm good."

"Dee," Brock shouts. "Forget everything I said. Just eat whatever you can until they kick us out."

"You're lucky," my dad says. "Some people never have one good friend. You've got three."

"Yeah. I know." I eat some more and then say, "You think all this snow is going to hurt the grass we planted out back?"

He shakes his head. "But if spring comes and it's patchy, we'll just put down some more seed."

"Right."

We sort of catch each other looking at the empty seat.

"I just—" I say, but a waiter puts more meat platters in our faces and of course we take some.

The main restaurant gets full and loud and everywhere is the smell of incredible food. I see Ellen reach for my dad's hand and confirm that the Great Red Spot has stopped raging for good. Then the waiters burst in with this incredible cake, candles lit, and they're singing and clapping and headed right for Misty. She's clapping with them—she's standing on her chair and conducting them like a choir director. They love it and go into another verse and then we all sing the regular happy birthday song. Misty blows the candles out like a boss, then presents appear. Most of them are gift cards or money toward one of the ridiculous things from her old Buffet List. Coffee comes and people start yawning and checking watches because we've been here for like three hours, but nobody leaves. They just keep digging at the cake or sipping water. Brock is trying to lie down on an empty chair. Max chucks rolled-up straw wrappers at his head.

There's this calm over everything, like this was the perfect night and we could all just go home and say it was epic and be done with it.

But there's this weird sense too that things aren't done. Like that grass we planted where the shed was out back—something has to spring up to cover what was there before. To close it out for good. So everybody knows we're living with the gaps and trying to get over it.

I stand up but bump the table, so the glasses clang and the dishes bang and a couple people look over. Now I'm standing for real, next to the empty throne, my hand on its back, looking down the gigantic table. Everybody is stopping their conversations. Brock sits up—they're all sitting up. Straight, like they were waiting for some kind of closure. I look at Claudia and she nods.

"Uh," I say. "Okay." Dead quiet. I do some quick math in my head. "Four hundred and some days ago, Misty came over to borrow some gas for her dad's mower. It was the day we found out about my mom. That She'd been killed." I land on Claudia again. She gives me this tiny smile.

"About a month later, Misty got sick," I say. Her parents look at each other. I see her dad reach over and grab Misty's hand. "I didn't remember that. And to be honest I didn't really care." That stings, bad. But it's true. I needed to say it. "I was sort of lost in my own thing. Brock and Tommy could tell you about that. My dad and sister too. Probably everybody. Really, I was a pretty bad friend and brother. Basically I was a Real Big Jerk to most people."

My voice shakes a little, and I take a second to steady it.

"It's pretty cool that Misty's birthday is a day after my mom's. It's really cool, actually. I think my mom would love to share Her party with somebody who is such a good friend to me. I think She would say, 'That Misty is a little off. And she's *awesome.*'"

People start clapping and Misty gets up on her throne doing the Middle Ages bow with the really low head and wide hands. She waves me over to stand with her, but I shake my head, so she yells something at Brock and Tommy and they drag me over. Misty hauls them up too and now we're all standing on this giant throne thing, holding on to each other so we don't fall off as people take a million pictures. She raises her glass toward the empty throne at the far end and everybody looks down the table at it. The room goes sort of quiet.

"Happy birthday, Mom," I say.

THE END
OF THIS
BOOK

AUTHOR'S NOTE

I wrote this book because I love postapocalyptic stories. But other people already wrote a ton of good ones, so I had to dig elsewhere. What I found was actually two stories, both somewhat taken from my classroom.

Twelve years teaching middle school has brought me a few Derricks and Mistys—kids who have lost a parent or survived a potentially fatal illness. I wanted to tell you about them. I wanted to write a story—perhaps not *their* specific one—where you might imagine their situation. Where you could feel what it might be like, as Derrick calls it, "to live with the gaps." Where you could see their struggles and strengths and ability to *go on* despite having stared down the barrel of The End. I will tell you that they amaze me, these thirteen-year-old survivors, who shoulder unbelievably heavy loads. They teach us all about true suffering. They teach us all to live differently.

But this is still a story, and therefore not meant to speak for survivors of parental loss or serious illness. As any clinical therapist will tell you, trauma impacts everyone differently. I am grateful to the mental health professionals who offered guidance on the story, specifically Liz Kornberg and Katie Hurley, as well as the therapists who have sat across from me on many a couch.

I did a lot of pushups while writing this book. I also found myself stockpiling water in my basement because North Korea was threatening their EMP strike again, and I'd read a book about what that would do and I was totally freaked out. Like Derrick, I live with anxiety; once I considered stopping this project. But then my wife reminded me of all the cognitive behavioral therapy exercises I'd spent money to learn, and things got better. You should check those out, they're really good. Also I prayed a lot, because God has a lot to say on the subject of worrying—notably, that he's near to the brokenhearted and those trapped by worries. People like me. Maybe like you.

ACKNOWLEDGMENTS

A lot of incredible people made this book possible. My wife, Kristy, acts as the great balancer of this whole writing thing; more than once the themes and deadlines of this project turned me into a Real Jerk, and she offered grace instead of wrath—a skill I am still honing. My agent, Lauren Galit, deserves lots of credit for this book too. She's that sort of agent who is really your first editor, and she stewarded this story the whole way. Enormous credit lies with my editor at Dial, Dana Chidiac, who both greenlit this project and then helped me age it down to make the story sing for my audience. Dana has this ability to ask the exact right question that doesn't just diagnose a narrative problem, but leads to a solution. It's fairly amazing, and my stories are better because of her guidance. And you must know about Regina Castillo. She has a PhD in catching minute errors during copyediting—she rules. I am also grateful to Lauri Hornik, el jefe in chief, for offering both insight to the story and a home for it at Dial, and all the staff who had a hand in Derrick and Misty's story, including Nancy Mercado, Mina Chung, Tony Sahara, Kristin Boyle, Tabitha Dulla, Ashley Spruill, and Carmela Iaria and her team.

I annoyed two medical experts pretty frequently: my sister-in-law, Helen Rominiecki, a transplant nurse, who provided meticulous detail on the kidney disease known as familial FSGS (focal segmental glomerulosclerosis) that Misty survived, and my friend Julia Pray, who worked as a nurse in the Pediatric ICU at Children's Hospital of Philadelphia where Misty was treated. Likewise, I consulted two service members on military matters: my sister, Dr. Sarah Wilson (Major, USAF), and my friend Dr. Trevor Smith (Major, USAF). Both have been spared deployments, and thus shielded their families from the specific trauma that Derrick endured. Many other military families have not been so fortunate. They live in the gaps daily.

Finally, I need to thank school guidance counselors everywhere, specifically my friend and colleague Jeff Klein, who answered my many guidance-related questions with spreadsheet precision. Jeff and his people walk with students under these heavy circumstances, supporting and seeking their ultimate good—all of which allows them to learn when they get to the classroom. As a teacher, but mainly as a dad, I am glad there are guidance counselors like Jeff. I pray that my kids never need him like Derrick did, but should they, it will be to their ultimate good.